ROMANCING
THE KING

ROMANCING
THE KING

•

Jocelyn Saint James

AVALON BOOKS
NEW YORK

Published by Thomas Bouregy & Co., Inc.
160 Madison Avenue, New York, NY 10016

Library of Congress Cataloging-in-Publication Data

Saint James, Jocelyn.
   Romancing the king / Jocelyn Saint James.
      p. cm.
   ISBN 978-0-8034-9932-4 (hard cover : acid-free paper)
1. Women physicians—Fiction.   2. Elvis Presley
impersonators—Fiction.   I. Title.

   PS3619.A398R66 2009
   813'.6—dc22

                                          2008031617

PRINTED IN THE UNITED STATES OF AMERICA
ON ACID-FREE PAPER
BY HADDON CRAFTSMEN, BLOOMSBURG, PENNSYLVANIA

To my husband, Jim—my king.

You show to me
When you sing,
Whom I could be
If you were my king.

Chapter One

"Elvis Presley is waiting in Exam Room Three."

Dr. Lindsey Bartlett looked up from the chart Nurse Mary Hollingsworth had just handed her. "What?" she asked, sure the bustling emergency room and the adrenaline rush she was feeling had skewed the message.

"You heard me right, Doctor. Elvis Presley is waiting for you in Exam Room Three." Mary's face grew red as she tried unsuccessfully to contain the chuckle erupting from her lips.

"Mary, this is no time for a joke. Very funny." Lindsey turned on her heels and marched into Exam Room Three of the Owl Cove General Hospital ER. Sure, she was always ready for a little fun, but doctoring and fun didn't always mix. And in her professional opinion, with the place overflowing with more patients than they could handle, now wasn't the time for fun.

Lindsey's shift in the ER had begun on an unusually easy note. *Maybe, just maybe, this would be a day filled with typical lacerations, bee stings, and simple fractures*, she thought. Considering the beautiful June weather and the abundance of pollen in central New York, she'd even be willing to throw in a few allergy attacks. In Owl Cove, snuggled comfortably on the eastern corner of Lake Ontario, at least once a week during the summer someone tripped on the slippery rocks on the lakeshore, twisting an ankle or breaking a toe. That, she was also prepared to handle.

No such luck. By nine o'clock that morning, just an hour after her shift had begun, the day had insane written all over it. *Batten down the hatches and get ready to rumble,* she told herself as she hurried from room to room, wiping the perspiration from her brow and tucking her springing curls behind her ears. She'd already seen a dog bite, a fall from a roof, and a toddler who'd stuck M&Ms up his nose. A busload of people who were bumped and bruised when their tour bus collided with the town's oldest oak tree hovered anxiously. Fortunately, a few bandages and cold compresses were enough to take care of that crew.

The ER was abuzz and, for some odd reason, Mary was apparently in a joking mood. Not too appropriate considering the circumstances and, actually, out of character for Mary. Elvis. What was she thinking?

Lindsey pushed her horn-rimmed glasses up on her nose and took a quick look at the clipboard in her hands. Jason Kincaid, twenty-nine years old, suspected pulled-back muscle. Blood pressure: normal. Respiration: normal. Temperature: normal. From all accounts, this case looked to be, well, normal.

She spoke as she walked into Exam Room Three, not looking up from the chart. "Hello, Mr . . ." She smiled and raised her eyes to a man in a red jumpsuit complete with bell-bottom pants and wide-lapelled collar. A gold pendant hung on a heavy chain around his neck. His jet-black hair and long sideburns had that distinctive look of the one and only Elvis Presley. He stood near the exam table, reaching under the wide-sequined belt with the enormous buckle to rub the small of his back.

". . . Mr. Elvis . . . ah, Mr. Presley." Lindsey shook her head and pursed her lips, disturbed at her inability to contain her error. She looked back at the chart. "Mr. Kincaid"—Lindsey corrected quickly and smiled as she felt the heat of embarrassment rush to her cheeks— "I'm Dr. Bartlett." She tried not to stare or giggle. Just as Mary had said, Elvis Presley—or at least a close replica—was here. In Exam Room Three.

Jason forced a pained smile and then winced as he continued to rub his back.

Lindsey gently placed her hand on his arm and led him to a chair. Carefully she helped him lower onto the seat, and he let out a little yelp.

"Okay, Mr. Kincaid?" She patted his shoulders.

"The hard part is over. Just relax and let me take a look."

"I think I'll live," Jason said, forcing a smile.

Although he didn't have a crooked little grin like Elvis, his smile was no less charming. His broad jaw and straight nose were also uniquely his own. The twinkle in his eyes had that Elvis magic. But the tar-black wig—well, the hair was all Elvis.

"That's what a doctor wants to hear." Lindsey pulled a pen from the breast pocket of her white coat. "So tell me what's going on with your back? What brings you to this fun place?"

"I was doing a show at the Cooper Senior Center," Jason began, taking a deep breath as the pain flared up. "I'm an Elvis Presley impersonator, by the way."

"Really?" Lindsey asked with a little grin. Under her glasses, her eyes darted from Jason to her clipboard and back to Jason as she wrote notes. Good, an impersonator. At least he wasn't some crazy guy who thought he really was Elvis. She wouldn't have to recommend psychiatric treatment.

"When I got to the part where I gyrate my hips to 'Jail House Rock,' you know . . ." He attempted the smallest display of the fatal movement . . . and his face crumpled in pain.

"Easy," Lindsey admonished, placing her hand on his shoulder. "I get the idea."

"When I got to that part," Jason continued, "some little old lady—no bigger than a hundred pounds—flew out of her chair, ran to the front of the room, and jumped on me, hanging around my neck like a squirrel dangling from a tree."

Lindsey tried to suppress a snicker. She reminded herself that this was her patient talking, not Elvis himself, although the stunning resemblance made it hard to separate the two—at least visually. This case may have an intriguing air of amusement, but before her sat a man in pain. And to a physician, that trumped everything.

"She caught me off balance. I didn't want to fall on her, so I twisted and let her fall on me." Jason rubbed his back again and sighed. "We both ended up on the floor."

"Well, that was quite heroic." Lindsey pushed her pen behind her ear to free up her hands. She pulled Jason slightly forward and pushed and thumped on his lower back, assessing his reaction with each gentle move.

"And how's the little old lady?" she asked, smiling more widely than she should have.

"That crazy granny is just great," said Jason sarcastically. "She grabbed my scarf and ran out of the room while I rolled around on the floor, barely able to move. I could hear her squealing to her friends that she got Elvis's scarf. Those ninety-year-olds can be tough!" He laughed then tightened in pain.

"How well I know." Lindsey slowly moved Jason upright in the chair, had him raise his arms, made him turn right and left, and asked him a dozen questions. She wrote some more notes and then looked at him directly, wondering if those deep-brown eyes, unusual for someone with such a fair complexion, were the result of contact lenses or just another characteristic that made him so unique.

"Well, I think you just have a pulled muscle. We'll do an x-ray to make sure. Hold tight, and someone will be in to take you to X-ray, Mr. . . ." She looked again at his chart, fighting the urge to call him Elvis. ". . . Kincaid."

She winked at him as she did to all of her patients and left the room. Back at the nurses station, Lindsey handed Jason's chart to Mary. "Call for someone to take the patient in three to X-ray."

Mary's chubby cheeks immediately broke into a smile. "You mean Elvis?"

Lindsey nodded, remembering her professional demeanor. "Mary, please," she admonished gently. "This place is already insane enough without you stirring the pot."

Mary leaned over the desk, close to Lindsey, so no one could hear. "So Lind . . . is he for real?"

"Well, he's obviously not the *real* Elvis," she replied, a touch of sarcasm in her voice. She twisted her lips.

"A couple of the nurses from ICU want his autograph."

"For goodness' sakes!" Lindsey slapped the countertop. "What is it with these people? He's our patient. This is a hospital, not a nightclub." She raised an eyebrow, widened her eyes, and lowered her voice. "Call me when Elvis is out of X-ray."

An hour later as Lindsey zoomed out of Exam Room Six, her hands and white coat splattered with the plaster from a cast she had just applied, Julie, a thin nurse from Pediatrics, caught up with her quick stride. Lindsey didn't slow down.

"No," Lindsey said as Julie opened her mouth to speak.

"No, what?" asked Julie, bustling alongside of Lindsey.

"No, you can't have his autograph. No, there will be no pictures. No, I don't know where his next show is."

Julie shrugged and stopped while Lindsey continued without missing a step. Since word of Jason Kincaid's arrival had spread like wildfire through the small community hospital, she'd been barraged with one Elvis-crazy fan after another. And she just didn't understand. To a twenty-eight-year-old woman, Elvis Presley was just a legend, someone worshipped by the previous generation, a tabloid story of a ghost that still roams around the streets of Memphis, an overdone impersonator in some casino. Lindsey was amazed at the number of people in this hospital—young, old, male, female— who were die-hard Elvis fans and who apparently had a problem differentiating the real thing from Jason Kincaid. She'd even had to ask security to remove a handful of neighborhood people who were gathering outside to catch a glimpse of Elvis or Jason or whoever he was.

"Doctor," Mary said as Lindsey hurried by the nurses station, "Mr. Kincaid is back in Three." Mary shot Lindsey a mischievous glance and held up his chart. "Time to shake, rattle, and roll."

Lindsey huffed, snatched the chart from Mary's

hands, and headed to Jason's room. She scowled at four cafeteria workers who huddled outside of the room, craning their necks to see through the slit in the door.

"Okay, Mr. Kincaid, let's see what we have here," she said as she walked through the door. As she studied the series of x-rays posted on the lightboard, out of the corner of her eye she noticed a man with a short, gray, brush cut and a salt-and-pepper mustache. He wore jeans, a plaid shirt, and cowboy boots.

"Doctor," the man said in a slow drawl, nodding his head and smiling in a genteel southern manner.

"This is Bernie Dexter, my manager," Jason said.

"Hello, Mr. Dexter." Lindsey smiled and then quickly turned to the x-rays. She pulled her glasses from her pocket, propped them on her face, and studied the films carefully, bouncing from one to the other. She heard Jason and Bernie chattering about a show Jason was scheduled to do tomorrow.

"So what do you think, Doc?" asked Bernie, his voice filled with concern. "How is this boy?"

Lindsey turned toward Jason. "Good news. No breaks or anything out of alignment. Looks like you have a simple pulled muscle. Take some ibuprofen, apply cold compresses for a couple of days, and then apply heat as needed." She lowered her gaze and looked at Jason over the top of her glasses. "And no more hip thrusts and gyrations until the soreness is gone. Completely gone."

"But, Doctor," Jason said, slowly raising himself out

of the chair, "I have a show tomorrow night at the Boat House. A fortieth high school reunion." He reached for his back and groaned.

Lindsey crossed her arms and stiffened her stance. "Mr. Kincaid," she said sternly, "if you don't take it easy until that muscle heals, you'll end up really hurting yourself. And if that happens, it will take much less than a hundred-pound granny to take you down."

A look of disappointment washed over his face.

"Can't you just sit in a chair and sing?" she asked.

Bernie laughed, and Jason gave her a you-must-be-kidding look. "Without the moves, Elvis is just not . . . well . . . just not Elvis," Jason said. "Everyone knows The King is all about the moves."

Lindsey placed a gentle hand on Jason's shoulder. Apparently, not everyone. "My concern is for you, Mr. Kincaid, my patient. Elvis will have to figure things out for himself." She winked and left the room.

"That's just great, Bernie," Jason said with disgust as he straightened his collar high around his neck and prepared to leave the exam room. "I hate to cancel the show tomorrow and disappoint those people."

Bernie folded his arms and gave Jason a no-nonsense look. "Now you heard the good doctor. I can call that Elvis impersonator from Syracuse. It's just an hour away. Maybe he's available."

"I know; I know. It's just that—"

Bernie held up his hands, sun-aged twiggy fingers on

his calloused palms. "It's just that you got your sights set on somethin', and you're bein' too pig-headed to follow doctor's orders."

Jason sighed deeply, relenting to Bernie's scolding. Bernie, old enough to be Jason's father, never hesitated to dole out advice and chastise him when needed even though, technically, Jason was his boss.

"You're right. Dr. Bartlett knows her stuff. At least she has me believing her." And she has the most fabulous red curls and grass-green eyes I've ever seen, he wanted to add. "I'm just a small-town Elvis impersonator, not a doctor." His tone was defeated.

"And if you want to be more than small town, you need a good back," Bernie said. "C'mon. Time for The King to go home."

At eight o'clock that evening, an exhausted Lindsey sat on the swing on her front porch. Jingle, the black-and-white greyhound she adopted two years ago was curled in a ball on the floor. And Lily, the tortoiseshell cat whose tail had been shortened when a careless previous owner shut it in the car door, lounged lazily on Lindsey's lap.

Dozing in the padded chaise just a few feet away was her grandfather, Tom Bartlett. Lindsey and the eighty-nine-year-old man still lived in the same house they'd shared since she was four years old. She looked around—this was her life. Grandpa, animals, creaky porch swing. Exhaustion after a high-speed day in the

ER and relief that she'd been able to leave when her shift normally ended.

With the portable phone in one hand and her list of patients in the other, Lindsey proceeded to do what she did each night: phone the patients she had treated that day in the ER and check on their progress. A couple of the other doctors told her she was going way above and beyond, but she didn't care. She had always wanted to be a physician because she loved taking care of people, making sure they were well, easing their pain and anxiety. She never felt her duties stopped when her day shift ended. Even though she was usually able to leave the hospital at a reasonable hour, her profession meant that when her patients needed her, she was there for them, day or night. She was a doctor every minute of her life. The practice of medicine was her heart and soul.

So each night, surrounded by two needy animals Lindsey had adopted and a beloved grandfather whose lifeline she was happy to be, her work continued.

She looked at her list. Twenty-six people. Busy day at the hospital. Although Jason Kincaid's name was fifth, she decided to save him until last. His presence had turned her ER on end, but she couldn't shake her thoughts of the man with the dazzling smile, gentle demeanor, outlandish costume, and quirky profession. She couldn't help wondering just who he was under the garb. The man who took a hit to save an old woman. The man who, through his pain, managed a smile for all the autograph hounds and rubberneckers. He seemed to have more going on than just pretending to be a dead entertainer.

After the twenty-fifth call, she stretched the tired muscles in her neck, sighed, and dialed Jason's number. "Mr. Kincaid?" Lindsey asked when Jason answered. Who else did she expect would pick up his phone? A wife or girlfriend perhaps?

"Dr. Bartlett," Jason said immediately, his tone upbeat.

"Mr. Kincaid, I'm just making a *routine call* to see how your back is feeling."

"Sure is nice of you to think of me."

Lindsey was surprised he actually sounded happy to hear from her. Most people cringed when a doctor called them.

"So, how's the back?"

"Pretty good, actually. I've been taking it easy, just like you said."

She wondered if he was still wearing the tight red jumpsuit. That, she figured, could cut off his circulation and cause all kinds of other complications. "That's good to hear. Rest is the best thing."

"Say, Doctor," Jason began sheepishly, "if I keep feeling better, and if, you know, I make some miraculous recovery overnight . . . think it would be okay for me to . . . to do my show tomorrow?"

"No!" she snapped. "Even if you can swing your hips to the moon and back, you are *not* to perform tomorrow."

"Okay, okay. Hey, it never hurts to ask," Jason replied,

frustrated. "I probably sound like your kids—asking and asking until you say yes."

"Well, if I had kids, I'm sure they'd sound that way." She glanced at her grandfather, whose head bobbed as he slept until he woke himself up when his little snorts reached a crescendo. Throughout the years his pleas for cigars, chocolate, and another chance to drive the car reminded her of a child who tried his best to beat the system. Then she looked at the pets whose doe-eyed expressions often weaseled too many treats out of her. So, yes, in a way she did have kids: They were just geriatric and four-legged.

"Oh. Well, if you had kids, you'd be a great mom," Jason quickly added. "You sure took good care of me today."

Lindsey was surprised to hear his compliment. Sure, her patients often thanked her, but it was usually an afterthought as they hurried out the door, all too eager to be going home, running from her and the inherent unpleasantness of a hospital. Quite frankly, she didn't blame them. Her grandfather had always told her a doctor is the best friend everyone doesn't want to see.

"Just doing my job." Lindsey tried to keep her tone professional despite the comfortable feeling that talking to Jason evoked. "I . . . I hope you have someone at home who can help you." Hmm, she hadn't noticed Jason's marital status on his chart.

"Bernie said he'd stay, but I told him not to bother. I'm used to taking care of myself."

Lindsey admired Jason's self-sufficiency. She had always thought she, too, would be content by herself. But now that the end of her twenties was looming, she wasn't so sure. Sure, she had her work, her grandfather, and her best friend and colleague, Mary, but there was a loneliness she couldn't deny. Despite all of the people, pets, and patients in her life, she was, in a very odd way, alone.

"Well, be careful," she added. "And if you don't feel like your old self in a couple of days, call your doctor."

"But . . . I thought *you* were my doctor." Jason sounded puzzled.

"Don't you have a regular physician?"

"Well, no. I mean, I've never really gotten sick since I moved here last year. Sure, I've had my share of bumps and bangs but nothing too bad. No need for a doctor."

"Until today," Lindsey added, her tone mildly scolding. So that's why she didn't remember Jason from high school, although, according to his chart, he was just a year older than she was. He was a transplant to Owl Cove. Interesting. People tended to move away from, not into, Owl Cove. The small town didn't offer tons of business opportunities for young career people or any big-city excitement. No, living in Owl Cove meant a peaceful, small-town existence. Serene to some and boring to others.

"No comment," he said with a resigned chuckle. "Like Bernie said, the doctor is always right!"

"I knew there was a reason I liked Bernie," she said with a laugh that jolted Lily awake.

The cat let out a loud meow followed by a motorboat purr, and Lindsey stroked her stubby tail.

"Do I hear a cat?"

"That's Lily. I've disturbed her twenty hours of beauty sleep."

"So you're a cat person."

"And a dog person. How about you? Any pets?"

"Never. Growing up, uh, the situation was . . . uh . . . never right. And now I guess I'm too busy with . . . with things."

Lindsey sensed the hedge in his voice, making him sound vulnerable and almost . . . wounded. He sure didn't sound like Elvis or at least what she thought the real Elvis—confident and assertive—would have sounded like. And she didn't sound like Scarlett O'Hara, whom she dressed like once for Halloween, Lindsey reminded herself. She laughed silently at the absurdity to think that she, like the rest of this town, was beginning to define Jason by his alter ego. There was way more to this man than the dead celebrity he mimicked.

"Maybe someday you'll get a pet," she said, sensing she should remember her role as a physician and close the conversation, even though she would have preferred to chat. "Well, okay, Mr. Kincaid, I'll let you go rest. Any questions before I hang up?"

"Just one: What do I have to do to get you to be my doctor?"

Chapter Two

"Lindsey, we're really happy you're spearheading this campaign. Someone with your determination to help see the Owl Cove Long-Term and Geriatric Care Center come to fruition is a real benefit to everyone," said Henry Conrad, the hospital CEO. Through coffee-stained teeth that gapped in the front, he smiled at Lindsey, who sat in the chair across from his desk. "We need more dedicated doctors like you, Lindsey."

From the inflection in Henry's voice when he paged Lindsey that morning, she could sense he had called her into his office to do more than sing her praises. She braced herself.

Henry put his hands together and drummed his fingertips, finally placing his index fingers at the base of his lips. "But the unfortunate truth is that in three months

I need to give a complete financial report to the board of directors. If they don't see that we've raised a sufficient amount of money to break ground on this project, they'll give it the thumbs-down." He lowered his thumbs like a Roman gladiator. "So as committee chairperson, you need to step up the fundraising efforts; see what we can do to pad the coffers for this most worthwhile cause. It's all up to you, Lindsey. It's all up to you."

Lindsey caught her breath. When she agreed to take on this project a year ago, she had grandiose ideas of a place—a home really—where those needing long-term care and the elderly could go. She thought of Rebecca Hanover, the fifty-five-year-old mentally challenged woman who still lived with her elderly and feeble mother. And then there was Mrs. Walker, wife of the late reverend. She was diabetic and becoming more and more forgetful. She didn't even want to think of the dark fate that could befall Lionel Rhodes, the disabled Vietnam veteran, if his partner abandoned him.

And, of course, there was always Tom. When Lindsey first heard of the hospital's desire to establish the care center, the first thought she had was of her grandfather. She had no plans to relocate him from their home, but she was also his only relative. If something were to happen to her, what would become of him? Or what if his condition worsened so she couldn't keep him at home? Her practical side wanted to ensure Tom would be cared for, no matter what. She had a selfish reason to see this care center became a reality.

"So what are the next steps?" asked Lindsey, wringing her hands together. "How can we keep the ball rolling?"

"Well, as committee chair, that's up to you," Henry replied. "You and your people can decide what we need to do. But whatever you decide, understand it has to happen quickly and be effective. Time is of the essence, as is money. This is in your hands, Lindsey." Henry gestured with reaching arms.

And what if she couldn't raise the money? What then? Lindsey pushed the thought from her mind. No, failure just wasn't an option. The future of too many people depended on her ability to get her committee to come up with some fundraising ideas, to make money to establish the care center. She had to make this happen.

When Lindsey left Henry's office, her mind was spinning. With a never-ending parade of patients, Tom, the pets, and now the pressure of getting her committee to raise what seemed like a treasure trove, her already busy days—and nights—had just gotten busier. She headed immediately to the doctors' lounge to send an email to the committee.

To: Mary Hollingsworth, Julie Baines, Sanjay Patel, Enrique Dominguez
From: Lindsey Bartlett
Subject: Emergency Meeting of Care Center Committee
   Everyone, Henry told me we have three months to give the board of directors a positive financial report for the fundraising progress of the care cen-

*ter. We have to step things up, big time. Let's meet
Monday at noon in the cafeteria so we can brain-
storm over lunch. I really need your input. Thanks.
P.S. Lunch is on me.*

Lindsey pushed the send button and took a deep
breath. Three months! What at first seemed like the impossible was beginning to seem like the ridiculous. She
had faith the committee members would rise to the occasion and do their best. Already they'd proven to be a
mighty force when push came to shove. But were they
miracle workers? Well, they were committed to saving
lives every day, so that was a miracle as far as she was
concerned. If they couldn't do it, it couldn't be done.
Onward and upward.

The committee had some real heavy hitters. She
could always count on Mary, her best friend and chief
ER nurse, to step up to the plate. They first met in the
Owl Cove High School Library Club, also known as
"the club for cheerleader rejects." Drawn together by
their love of books, lack of coordination, and mouth
full of metal, the girls formed an enduring bond. Even
when they left town to go to separate colleges, they still
remained close.

Julie Baines was the middle-aged nurse from Pediatrics who, Lindsey found out yesterday, had a collection of Elvis memorabilia and was seeking a little
connection with the next best thing—Jason Kincaid.
Julie, a single mother of three, had a heart of gold and a

soft spot for anyone who needed help. Even though she ate like a horse, her nervous energy kept her metabolism running at warp speed. She remained thin as a rail and her wispy puff of brown hair was a common sight as she buzzed around the hospital. The committee needed someone with her stamina. Plus, maybe Julie could help Lindsey understand all the mystique surrounding Elvis. This situation with Jason in her ER had piqued her curiosity. Who knows: if she ever ran into Jason on the street, she'd need some material for small talk.

Sanjay Patel, head of facilities, was the one person who had his pulse on the operation of the entire hospital. Sanjay was a master at organization and kept everyone on track. He had a good head for money and a practical approach. Besides, during their meetings his wife often sent over Indian delicacies that were to die for. Since cooking wasn't Lindsey's forte, the treats were a welcome reprieve from the Oreos and potato chips Lindsey served.

Dr. Enrique Dominguez, Owl Cove's resident general surgeon, was a small man with a big heart and an abundance of enthusiasm. Having come to the area from his native Madrid just a year earlier, he was eager to share his talent, knowledge, and poor performance of flamenco guitar. He wanted to be an integral part of the community, and being involved in fundraising for the care center gave him the chance to do just that.

Lindsey glanced at the clock on the wall. Five sixteen. Late again. She needed to hurry home and give

Tom his dinner and medication. Fortunately, she could usually schedule her shift to accommodate her obligation to her grandfather. She'd already put in a nine-hour day, counting the twenty minutes she took at noon to run home and make sure Tom was eating the tuna fish sandwich she had left for his lunch. Living only two blocks from the hospital had its privileges.

Lindsey turned off the computer and walked over to her locker. She hung up her white coat and took a quick glance in the small mirror hanging on the inside of her locker door. She had dark circles under her eyes, and the lipstick she'd reapplied after eating the granola bar she called lunch had long since disappeared. Fortunately she'd be home soon and could change out of her skirt and blouse into her favorite pair of soft, faded jeans. She hesitated, wondering if she should stop by the lab and verify they'd ordered those test kits for her. No, that would have to wait until tomorrow. She grabbed her purse, closed her locker, and headed toward the exit via the ER.

As she stepped outside, Lindsey heard a voice call from the parking lot.

"Doctor! Doctor!"

She looked up to see Bernie balancing a hobbling Jason, in full Elvis regalia, toward the ER entrance.

"Doctor, Jason's foot," Bernie called.

Lindsey hurried over to the men and flung Jason's free arm over her shoulder. "Mr. Kincaid, what happened?"

They limped into the ER like a three-headed monster.

Lindsey and Bernie guided Jason to a chair in the hallway.

"I think I broke a toe," said Jason, his face twisted in pain.

Lindsey looked down at Jason's bare right foot and saw a swollen and black pinkie toe. When she touched it, he let out a yelp, similar to the sound Jingle made the time Tom caught his nose in the cupboard door. "So how did this happen?" she asked. "I thought you were going to lay off the performing for a while. You know, doctor's orders." She raised an eyebrow while she grabbed Jason's wrist to take his pulse.

"He wasn't performin', Doc," Bernie interjected. "I saw to that."

The thought of Jason wearing his Elvis garb when he wasn't on stage befuddled Lindsey, and she had to force herself to focus on her patient's condition.

"I had a photo shoot for the newspaper," Jason explained. "I was trying to walk carefully so I wouldn't strain my back, and I caught my foot on the doormat when I let in the photographer. I saw stars!"

"Stars other than Elvis?" Lindsey couldn't hold back a snicker. She breathed a sigh of relief that Jason was in costume for a legitimate reason. The thought of him walking around his house like a Norma Desmond character, waiting for the audience to applaud as he lip synced to some old albums, made her shudder.

A small throng was beginning to gather, tittering and taking pictures with their camera phones. Mary, on her way out the door, stood on tiptoe to see over the crowd. She hit her temple with the heel of her hand. "Not again," she said to Lindsey.

Lindsey rolled her eyes.

Mary took a deep breath. "Can I help, Doctor?" The nurse was back on duty.

"Looks like a broken toe. Simple fracture. Can you have someone take Mr. Kincaid to X-ray?"

Mary gave a quick nod of her head and held up her index finger. "I know the drill," she said, heading back to the nurses' station.

Lindsey raised her hands in exasperation and asked the crowd to scatter after an overzealous man, scurrying from an exam room while holding closed the back of his hospital gown, asked Jason for an autograph. This was all too much!

"Told you that you had an effect on people," Bernie said to Jason with a proud smile.

"Not me, Elvis." "There's a difference." Jason stared down at his foot and wrinkled his nose. "Does that toe look like it's swelling more?"

Lindsey looked at his foot. "No difference in the condition of the toe. But is there really a difference between you and Elvis?" She was writing notes on a pad pulled from her briefcase.

Jason's face lit up. "Don't tell me I had you fooled, too, Doctor!"

"Just doing a reality check," she replied, relieved at his response. So this whole Elvis bit was really just an act—some fun way to make a living. She really didn't want him to be some kook who thought he was a reincarnated spirit. He seemed far too special.

"Elvis's eyes were really blue; mine are brown. Big difference." He turned to Lindsey, poker-faced.

She looked up from her pad, directly into his eyes. He had to be kidding. As she studied his expression, he cracked a wide smile and hissed out a laugh he was trying to hide. Hmm. She liked a good sense of humor, she thought as she, too, laughed.

"This the hurt guy, Doctor?" asked the orderly who came to wheel Jason to X-ray. "Don't see too many hurt guys laugh." The portly man hefted Jason into the wheelchair with an easy tug.

"That's him," said Lindsey, a laugh still trickling from her voice. "I'll be here when you return," she said to Jason as he was wheeled away. "Smile for the camera."

His face lit up. "You were on your way out. You're going to stay just for me?"

"Well, I am your doctor, aren't I?" She put her hands on her hips and tilted her head towards him.

"Always were, as far as I was concerned. Maybe now that I'm your *real* patient, you'll call me Jason instead of Mr. Kincaid." He waved as he was wheeled into the elevator.

Lindsey finished her notes, gathered her briefcase, and hurried out the door. If she took the shortcut by the convenience store on the corner, she'd be able to run home, take care of her grandfather, and hurry back to read Jason's x-rays. If she walked a little faster than usual, she'd even have time to freshen up her lipstick before she returned.

Something told her she hadn't seen the last of Jason Kincaid.

On the ride home from the hospital, Jason's broken toe throbbed under the bandage that anchored it to the neighboring toe. But that wasn't his concern. Elvis would just have to wear sneakers for a while. No, his toe wasn't the problem—the fact he couldn't get Lindsey out of his mind was. That beautiful doctor with a head full of soft red curls, green eyes that flashed like emeralds in sunshine, perfect figure, and angelic composure was unlike anyone he had ever met before. Smart, dutiful, and sweet. He suspected that underneath the serious demeanor and starched white coat was a good sense of humor and someone who needed more fun in her life. She'd actually waited after her shift for him. Cared for him as if he were more than just some two-bit performer who had stumbled into her ER—not an insignificant gesture. And definitely not a kindness anyone had ever extended to him before.

"Hate to tell you this," said Bernie as he turned his expansive, mint-condition, 1980 blue Lincoln Continental around the corner to Jason's apartment. "That gig at the sixtieth birthday party for next week was canceled. Seems the birthday gal decided to spend her money on Botox instead."

"That's just great," said Jason, pursing his lips. "Anything else to get in the way of my work? Pulled back, broken bones, and Botox. Maybe the demand for Elvis in this town is drying up." He leaned his head against the car window.

"Naah." Bernie reached over and grasped his arm, shaking it gently. "Elvis will never dry up. Long live The King. We just need to get you more exposure. I think there are lots of stones yet to be unturned in this town."

Jason drummed his knuckles on the window. "Sometimes I wonder if we'd be better off in a bigger city with more opportunities. A chance to do more than birthday parties and old folks' homes." He sat upright and leaned his head on the headrest. "No sense even thinking about that. I can't move now because of . . . well . . ."

Bernie pulled into the driveway of Jason's apartment house and stopped the car. "You just concentrate on healin' that toe. Leave the rest to me."

Chapter Three

Lindsey's neck and shoulder muscles melted under the penetrating heat of the midday sun, a thousand fingers massaging her tense muscles. The relaxation slowly quivered throughout her body. She was glad she decided to fall prey to Mary's coaxing and take Tom for a walk through the Harbor Festival, Owl Cove's annual summer event.

When she rose at six o'clock on that Saturday morning, her only day off for the week, Lindsey had intended to get an early start on formalizing some plans for the fundraising committee so she'd be ready for their meeting on Monday. She showered, threw on some cotton shorts and a T-shirt, grabbed a cup of herbal tea and her notebook, and headed to the porch swing to write her plans.

She flipped through the notebook, checking the minutes of the committee meetings, reading the many ideas that had already been done and those that had been scrapped. So much work had been completed, and yet there was so much more to do. She was overwhelmed by the magnitude of this undertaking. If she didn't make sure this care center was built, she'd be letting down so many people, including herself.

What could they do to really bring in some money? They've held bake sales, pledge walks, even pancake breakfasts where the doctors served. While those events were successful, the proceeds weren't sufficient to take their fundraising to the next level. Lindsey chewed the top of the pen and propped her foot on the railing to push the swing. Yard sale, she jotted down. Maybe all the hospital employees could donate their cast-offs to a gigantic yard sale to be held in the hospital parking lot. Good idea. Clam bake, Lindsey also wrote. Nothing says summer along Lake Ontario like a clam bake. Or how about some fun with a Hospital Idol show in the high school auditorium? Surely the townspeople would buy tickets to see the hospital staff make fools of themselves! Plus, that would be a way to wind down a little. Lately, she'd been consumed by obligations that seemed to be zapping the fun, the spontaneity out of her life. Maybe that dream she'd had the other night of throwing off her white coat and jumping, fully clothed, into a swimming pool was more prophetic than she thought and not just the result of too much salsa before bed.

Looking at her notes, she smiled. So far, so good. Already she was feeling better—more productive and hopeful she could maybe, just maybe, meet the demands of the board of directors. After writing some plans to get the yard sale and clam bake in motion, Lindsey congratulated herself and went into the house for another cup of tea. When the phone rang, she grabbed it quickly before it woke her grandfather.

"You're up early," Mary said over the phone. "I was afraid I'd wake you."

"I wanted to get a jump start on some of the fund-raising plans." Lindsey dunked her tea bag. "I'm getting nervous now that the heat is on. Tell me we can do this, Mare."

"Okay, I'll tell you. We can do it."

Lindsey bit her lip. "Wish you'd said that like you meant it."

"I do mean it, but we have a ton of work to do, Lind. The town really needs this care center. We're talking about raising some mega bucks. And face it, we're limited in resources."

Lindsey nodded, thinking of her grandfather. "I really need this care center too." She took a sip of tea, then cradled the phone between her head and shoulder, freeing up her hands to add a spoonful of honey. "Wish I could find that magic bullet that would make the difference."

"Keep looking. It's bound to show up when you least expect it."

"Sure hope so." Lindsey took another sip.

"So can I entice you to go to the festival? Thought I'd wander around after lunch."

"I'd like to," Lindsey started, her voice hesitant, "but . . ."

Mary interrupted. "I know; I know. But you're too busy. You have work to do."

"Give me a break, Mare," Lindsey retorted, aggravated. "This fundraising is eating at me." She leaned against the counter, enjoying the coolness of the linoleum on her bare feet.

"I hate to be the one to break this to you," said Mary, "but there's more to life than work. If you don't give yourself a break, have a little fun, you'll end up in that care center yourself, suffering from exhaustion. You sure won't find that magic bullet unless you start looking for it. And being stuck in the ER or the house all the time isn't the answer."

She sighed. Mary's words rang true. Lindsey was pushing too hard. She always did. Full weeks at the hospital, time with the fundraising committee, caring for Tom—she seemed to always have time for everyone and everything, except herself. Some fun, or, even better, someone to have fun with, would sure be nice.

"Doctors make the worst patients," Lindsey replied.

"Tell me something I don't know!"

Lindsey was reluctant, but she knew Mary was right. She needed a break—or she was going to break. "Okay, okay. How about if I put Grandpa in his wheelchair and meet you at the festival around one? By the dunk tank where we always meet."

"Keep your hat on, Grandpa." Lindsey maneuvered Tom's wheelchair through the crowd. "You'll get burned to a crisp in this sun."

"Feels good on these old bones," Tom said, shoveling some honey roasted peanuts into his mouth. "Sun hasn't hurt me in almost ninety years, and it isn't going to hurt me now!"

"I agree," said Mary. "Capture this feeling for those long, cold winter days." She pulled a barrette from her pocket and wound her chestnut hair into a knot on the back of her head.

"Are you wearing sunblock?" Lindsey asked her friend.

"Yes, Doctor," Mary replied sarcastically, eliciting a snippy glance from Lindsey. "SPF thirty if you must know."

"I'm wearing forty-five," Lindsey replied.

"Well, I don't have skin the color of milk, Miss Porcelain!" Mary replied, the snip in her voice infused with fun.

"You know how easily I freckle," Lindsey added with a flip of her head.

Tom surveyed the fairgrounds, casting a thoughtful eye on the carousel. "Why, I remember when your grandmother went on that carousel when she was just a teenager with a crush on a dapper guy." He pointed a shaky hand toward the colorful ponies that were circling to the up-and-down rhythm of the calliope.

"Would that guy be you?" asked Mary, reaching into Tom's bag of peanuts for a handful.

"Darn tootin'! I wore a straw hat and starched high collar. And Nellie, well, she was a showstopper with her red curls. Just like yours, Lindsey. Cute as a button!"

"You old dog," said Mary, giving Tom a playful poke on the shoulder that made him giggle.

They made their way through the festival, stopping to play a few games, eat candy apples and sugar waffles, and buy some Christmas tree ornaments at the holiday tent. When they reached the midway, Tom's face lit up like a child's.

"Did you get my ticket for the Ferris wheel?" he asked, his eyes opening wide at the site of the carnival icon.

Lindsey stretched her mouth into a toothy square. "Grandpa, look how high that is. I don't think you want to go on that, do you?"

"Sure do! I'm eighty-nine years old. Think I'm afraid of a Ferris wheel? Haaa! I fought in World War II!" He started to lift himself from his wheelchair.

Lindsey gently pushed him back down. "It's just that—"

"I know. *You're* afraid of heights. I'm not asking you to go with me. I'm certainly capable of taking a ride alone."

Lindsey lifted her hands in question to Mary. She

didn't want to stifle Tom's fun, but a Ferris wheel was no place for a man his age.

"Tell you what," Mary said to Tom, "you and I will take a spin on the wheel while Lindsey watches us have all the fun." Mary winked at Lindsey behind Tom's back, and Lindsey's shoulders sank in relief as she mouthed the words "thank you."

"Now you're talking," Tom said. "I like a girl with some adventure in her bones!"

"I'll wait over there." Lindsey gestured to the pavilion as Mary pushed the wheelchair towards the ride.

Lindsey bought a lemonade and sat on a bench. The outdoor seats were packed, and several people stood, clapping and laughing, exchanging greetings as only people who've been friends for years do. The town was alive, and everyone was enjoying the picture-perfect weather that was such a sharp contrast to the ferocious winters that Lake Ontario delivered.

For many months each year, Lake Ontario unleashed its fury on Owl Cove, pummeling everything and everyone with snow that was outrageous enough to put the sleepy little town on the national news and make it the brunt of jokes by the late night talk show hosts. Great waves were unleashed from the lake, plastering an icy coating on the shoreline and obliterating the breakwall from view. Each winter, Tom recalled the blizzards of '58 and '66, and seemed to wait for another record-setting snowfall to descend on the town. Everyone handled the weather with expert aplomb; but when spring and summer rolled around, the townsfolk were out and about, enjoying every minute and luxuriating in the warmth. Reaping the bounty for their months of hibernation.

Over the roar of the crowd, Lindsey heard Tom and Mary yell to her from high atop the Ferris wheel. She turned and waved to them as they tottered their seat back and forth, laughing in devilish delight when Lindsey cringed. Even without her glasses, she could see the thrill on her grandfather's face. If the sun weren't warming her, his look of joy would have.

Behind her Lindsey heard the crowd cheer. She craned her neck to see a distant stage surrounded by people jumping—literally jumping—up and down. The sounds from a twangy guitar matched the rock 'n' roll beat of a white-clad figure. She put on her glasses for a closer look. Elvis. Jason. Him! Lindsey tore off her glasses, jumped to her feet, and moved toward the stage.

As Jason came into focus, the crispness and tone of his voice also became clearer. Sounded like the real thing. Deep, resonating, a heartbeat rhythm that immediately appealed. With each accentuated movement, the crowd went wild. When Jason ripped the scarf from around his neck, wiped his brow, and flung the gossamer cloth into the crowd, sending it floating down into hundreds of hopeful hands, Lindsey thought a stampede had broken out. What was it about those scarves?

Wrapped tightly in a white jumpsuit studded with silver buttons, Jason swayed to the music, dipped and dove while his legs bent effortlessly in tandem from side to side as if he were made of rubber. Apparently, his back was feeling better. Lindsey looked at his feet. At least he was wearing sneakers to protect his broken toe! All body parts appeared to be in order.

It wasn't the frenzy of the crowd or the clarity of his voice or the be-bop sway of his body that caught her attention. It was his face. Serene and pure—absolutely pure—joy emanated from his soul and glowed on his face, making Lindsey catch her breath. That look was real. The gaudy costume, the wig, the persona—all of that was an entertaining put-on. But the joy on Jason's face was too real, too perfect, to be anything but genuine.

She was mesmerized. Caught in the fury, she, too, started to move from side to side with the music. No, she had never been an Elvis Presley fan. He was a legend from a bygone era, not even alive when she was born. To her generation, Elvis was a mystique that had become larger than the man himself probably ever was. In death, his popularity continued to grow to epic proportions. He held a coveted position at the top of the rock 'n' roll food chain, of that Lindsey was sure. But until she saw Jason, Elvis was just a collection of tabloid stories and songs from the oldies channel. An incarnation of the legend was right in front of her. And Lindsey was entranced.

"Packs quite a punch, don't he, Doc?" She turned to see Bernie standing behind her, a wide smile accentuating the creases at the side of his mouth.

"You could say that!" she said, unable to contain the excitement in her voice. "I never imagined Jason was such a talented performer."

Bernie nodded. "That boy has got what it takes. Knew it the first time I saw him."

Lindsey sensed the pride in his voice. She wasn't sure what 'what it takes' meant, but from what she saw, on stage and even in her couple encounters with Jason at the ER, she'd have to agree.

Bernie stood silently while Jason swayed effortlessly into another number. Jason looked over the crowd, his gaze freezing on Lindsey. He touched his back and gave her a high-five, causing her to smile widely. Then he lifted his sneaker-clad foot, formed his thumb and index finger into a circle, and flashed the a-okay sign. The doctor in her was relieved to see her patient doing so well. And the woman in her was melting underneath the touch of the gentle lyrics he crooned and the thousand-watt smile that rivaled even the bright sunshine.

"There you are." Mary pushed Tom's wheelchair beside Lindsey. "We were looking for you."

Lindsey pointed to the stage.

Mary stretched to see above the crowd, then she turned to Lindsey with her mouth agape. "It can't be!"

"I can't see a thing," Tom whined, rising slightly from his chair. "What's going on over there?"

"Just a guy pretending to be Elvis," Mary said.

"Just a guy," Lindsey added, her voice trailing off, eyes glued to the stage.

As Jason's song was about to end, Bernie tapped Lindsey on the shoulder. "Come with me." He led Lindsey, Mary, and Tom through the small line of security guards to behind the stage where they saw a trailer doubling as Jason's dressing room and the Garden Club's winter storage. "If Jason thought I let you get away, he'd have my hide." Bernie winked an eye weathered from years of sun and knocked on the door of the trailer. "People to see you."

Jason swung open the door and was refastening his red, white, and blue cape to his shoulder. His smile widened when he saw Lindsey. "And I thought it was just some fans." He stepped out of the trailer.

"We're fans," Lindsey said. "That was some show out there!" She fought the urge to hug him. If only she could treat him for something that required him to remove his costume so she could see the real Jason under the sequins and wig.

"Nice of you to say, Doctor," Jason said. His gaze magnetized to her.

"Lindsey," she replied, lowering her eyes a bit. "Call me Lindsey. After all, I *am* your doctor. First names are appropriate."

Mary nudged her friend, but Lindsey didn't respond.

"Jason, you know Mary from the hospital. And this is my grandfather, Tom Bartlett."

"Pleasure to see you again, Mary," Jason said, holding out his hand to her. "Especially a pleasure because I'm not being dragged before you on a stretcher!"

"Let's keep it that way," Mary chuckled. "I will say, you were the most popular patient we had in some time. Everyone loves Elvis!"

"I'll make sure to tell him that," Jason joked. He held out his hand to Tom. "Now here's a man who I bet will give me an honest opinion. Thanks for watching my show, Tom. How bad was I?"

"Well, I couldn't see much from down here with everyone jumping like they had ants in their pants!"

"We can't have that." Jason broke out into a quick rendition of "Teddy Bear," complete with dance moves. Lindsey and Mary moved to the tune and giggled like teenagers, clutching each others' arms. Lindsey never reacted like this to an Elvis song. Usually, she changed the radio station. Was it, perhaps, the singer?

Tom's eyes lit up, and he clapped with excitement. When Jason finished, Tom reached over and shook his hand. "I once knew a man who could wiggle his hips and shake his behind better than anyone in the county. The ladies used to swoon when he walked by. And his voice was smooth as silk. Lucky for you that man is sitting in this wheelchair or you'd have yourself some stiff competition on that stage!" Tom laughed so hard the wheelchair shook.

"Grandpa!" Lindsey tugged Tom's hat lower on his head. "Don't let all the family skeletons out of the closet! Not just yet anyway!" She winked at Jason. "I think he's still dizzy from that Ferris wheel ride."

"I don't think Elvis here would be any less sweet on you if I kept those skeletons hidden," Tom said.

As his forgetfulness had grown in recent years, so had his inability to restrain his thoughts. Lindsey felt her cheeks redden, and she stiffened as Jason smiled even wider, not at all daunted by Tom's words.

Mary nudged her again with her elbow.

"So, young fella," Bernie said to Tom. "Remember when Elvis was the hot ticket?"

Tom looked at Bernie with confusion. "Well, that's a bold statement to say when the man is standing right here!"

"No, I mean the real Elvis from the great, early days of rock 'n' roll."

Tom placed his hand to the side of his lips to shield his mouth from Jason as he replied to Bernie. "This *is* the real Elvis. The boy can hear you!"

Lindsey patted Tom's shoulder. "It's been a long day in the sun. I think it's time for us to head home so Grandpa can catch a little nap."

Jason nodded knowingly. "Tom, whenever you'd like Elvis to give you a private concert, you just let me know."

"Okay, pal," he said, as Lindsey turned around his chair to leave. "When you come calling on my granddaughter, I'll expect a song."

Lindsey placed her hand over her mouth as if the faux pas had just come from her instead of Tom.

Jason smiled and turned to her. "Elvis was never one to turn down an invitation."

Later that evening after Tom had gone to bed, Lindsey sat on the porch steps, her bare feet relishing the warm wooden boards as she gazed at the carpet of twinkling stars. She'd just finishing calling the hospital to check on some lab reports for two patients she had admitted earlier in the week when the phone, still in hand, rang.

"I found Tom's bag of peanuts in my tote," said Mary, not bothering to say hello. "I put them there when we went on the Ferris wheel. Thought he may be looking for them."

"Didn't mention them," Lindsey replied. "He must have forgotten."

"Or else he ate enough to last until next year's festival."

"That too. Between the nuts, the hot dogs, and the other junk, I thought for sure I'd have to give him something to settle his stomach. He must be tougher than I thought. Say, Mare," Lindsey said, her voice hesitating, "did you notice Grandpa thought Jason was the real Elvis?" She twisted her curls around her finger, stretching them out and letting them spring back, as she waited for Mary's reply.

"He's not?"

"Enough, Miss Comedian. This is serious. I'm worried about Grandpa. First the confusion about Elvis, then who knows what next. Just the other day he put salt in his coffee instead of sugar."

"He's almost ninety. All in all, he's doing great. You have to expect some confusion from time to time."

"I suppose." Her thoughts trailed to the care center and the safe haven it could be to Tom and so many others.

"The heat, the Ferris wheel, and the excitement of the show probably got the best of him," Mary said. "I'd say Elvis got the best of you too."

"Don't be silly," Lindsey added quickly. "Jason is my patient. It was just fun to watch him."

"If he looks half as cute in his street clothes as he does in costume, he definitely is a force to be reckoned with. Like him?"

Lindsey cleared her throat and twisted her hair tighter. "Of course, I like him. He's . . . he's my patient."

Mary laughed. "You're talking to me, Lind. You know, the one who's seen the look—*that* look—in your eyes ever since high school."

Lindsey unleashed the curls from her fingers and found it difficult to suppress the little grin that curled her lips. "Mary! Are you saying I have a thing for Elvis?"

"I'm just saying."

Chapter Four

"I can't believe I let you talk me into this." Lindsey huffed as they slipped into a booth at the Marina Pub.

"Didn't take much arm-twisting," Mary snipped, opening her menu and holding it high to block her view of Lindsey. "You sure seemed to enjoy his show at the festival yesterday."

Lindsey puckered her lips and blew the curls out of her eyes. "Is it a crime to like his music?" She pulled the straps of her pink sundress higher on her shoulders. "I happen to think the guy is a good singer," she added.

Mary lowered her menu and shot Lindsey a smug grin. "Better order before the show starts."

The Marina Pub, a quaint location on the lakeshore, welcomed boaters and anyone looking to enjoy a stint in the sun and absorb the moist, fresh lake air. The casual dining area encircled a center floor that held light entertainment such as karaoke, small ensembles, or a holiday choir. In the summer, the walls of the restaurant opened onto the lake, inviting an airy, romantic breeze that softly fluttered sleeves and made the patrons toss back their heads to soak it all in.

Lindsey and Mary placed their orders and chatted. Mary provided copious details about a movie she'd seen the night before. They watched the small restaurant fill with diners. And just as the waitress served Mary's grilled shrimp and Lindsey's Cobb salad, the show began.

Without fanfare, Jason walked to the center of the floor, picked up his microphone, and greeted the approximately one hundred diners and bar patrons with a quick, "Welcome to the Marina Pub. My name is Jason Kincaid. I hope to make you forget that and think about . . . The King."

Just then, the music resounded with a startling downbeat, and Jason broke into a lively rendition of "Don't Be Cruel." That song led seamlessly into a series of other Elvis favorites, complete with swaying, waving scarves, bending on one knee, outstretching arms, looking to the ceiling with dramatic head thrusts, and making eye contact with the patrons.

During a tamer song, Jason sauntered from table to table, presenting each guest with a private concert and draping a scarf around the necks of some women. When he approached Lindsey and Mary's booth, he did a double-take and the corners of his mouth lifted into a smile, even though "Glory, Glory Hallelujah" didn't call for any gestures of jocularity.

Lindsey's heart skipped a beat as Jason stood before her, his eyes riveted on her as he sang. He put his head back and belted out crystal-clear notes, and his hand gestured outward from his chest as if he were pulling the song from deep inside. When he reached those words meant to draw the breath from the audience, he closed his eyes and the deep, melodic reverberation of his voice almost echoed within her chest. Standing before her, Jason acted as if she were the only one in the audience.

She felt she was.

Mary was shaking with glee, and she tugged at Lindsey's dress from under the table. Lindsey didn't respond. She was bewitched by this man. Outwardly, inwardly, and in all other possible dimensions. She couldn't even pretend to be otherwise although she was totally shocked at her reaction.

As the song ended, Jason retreated, walking backward to the center of the room, his eyes never leaving Lindsey as the departing notes rolled from his lips, quieting as he backed away.

"He is so into you," Mary whispered. "I've never seen anything like it."

"Uh, huh," Lindsey responded vacantly, her eyes still locked on Jason.

"Did you see that? He didn't even try to be subtle!"

"Uh, huh." She heard Mary's words, but could offer no reply other than a mumble.

When the house lights turned on, Jason told the clapping crowd he'd return for the next set in a half hour. His eyes again scanned the crowd and stopped on Lindsey. A subtle smile and almost imperceptible lift of his eyebrows were delivered to her. Then he turned and walked through a door at the back of the dining area.

"So what was that all about?" asked Mary when the restaurant had quieted down and the diners had returned to their food.

"What was what about?" Lindsey rearranged the components of her Cobb salad but didn't take a bite.

Mary popped a shrimp into her mouth and spoke with her cheeks bulging. "I saw the way you two looked at each other. You'd have to be blind not to notice. Or dead not to feel it!"

Lindsey took a big gulp of water. "Come on, Mare. Feel what?"

"You tell me! Suddenly, this turned into the Jason-Sings-to-Lindsey Show." She rolled her shoulders.

Lindsey brushed away her comment with a flick of her hand. "Sure, he's cute, and he seems really sweet. But the guy dresses like Elvis. I mean, really. Doesn't that strike you as a little odd?"

"But he just dresses up for his act. Kind of like we wear white coats and scrubs for our act." She stabbed some carrots on her plate.

Lindsey pondered Mary's comment. "I suppose, but doesn't impersonating a celebrity seem like kind of a strange job for a guy to have? Why doesn't he get a real job?" She traced the drips of moisture on the outside of her water glass.

"Well, lots of people in Las Vegas and Hollywood make a fortune from impersonating the stars. Doesn't seem like it's any different from my Aunt Frieda who used to run that clown birthday party business." Mary wiped her mouth with the napkin.

"I hate to say it, but your aunt was a little cuckoo. I sure hope Jason's not like that. Do you think he always dresses in costume?"

"I doubt it. Why? Having fantasies about what the *real* Jason looks like?" Mary playfully kicked Lindsey's foot under the table.

Lindsey shook her head like a child clearing an Etch-A-Sketch to remove the image. Yes, she was having fantasies, but they were just gnats flying around her brain, like a tune to a jingle you just couldn't shake. "Time to change the subject." She dipped her fork in the cup of dressing, attacked a few leafs of lettuce, and took a bite. "I had some great money-making ideas for the care center," she said. "Let me run them by you before we meet with the committee tomorrow. I want your honest opinion."

"Have you ever known me to be anything but honest with you?"

"Well, just don't be cruel," Lindsey retorted playfully, catching herself as soon as the words were out of her mouth.

"Now you're talking the lingo!" exclaimed Mary. "Does he have your number or what!"

Lindsey gave a quick shake of her head and jumped right into her plans for the care center while they finished dinner and enjoyed the vista of the lighthouse on the lake. The scenery was peaceful as the gigantic red sun began its descent into the water and the chirp of seagulls swooping near the shore chimed the familiar sounds of summer on Lake Ontario. She wondered if Jason liked to sit on the lakeshore and watch the sun set. Why had she never run into him on the streets? She vaguely remembered seeing some posters over the last few months advertising Elvis shows, but she hadn't given them a second thought. That just wasn't her thing—or hadn't been anyway.

Just as the waitress was clearing away their dishes, the beat of the music signaling the start of Jason's second set kicked up in intensity, infiltrating the room and causing the crowd to clap in anticipation.

"Here we go," said Mary, her eyes twinkling as she turned toward the center of the room. "Get ready!" She rubbed her hands together.

"Oh, I'm ready," Lindsey said, the enthusiasm in her voice flat compared to her words. She put on her glasses. *Been ready for a long time*, she wanted to add.

As the music peaked, Jason entered from the same door he had exited earlier, the spotlight following him to the tall stool in the center of the room. He wore tight black leather trousers and a black leather jacket that shone in the reflection of the overhead lights. He had traded his white sneakers for black slip-on shoes to match the ensemble. A white silk scarf was draped loosely around his neck. In the form-fitting black costume, he looked like the bad boys her grandfather had always told her to stay away from, those boys who would turn out to be nothing but trouble.

Her grandfather had been wrong.

Jason raised his hand to the crowd and pivoted three hundred and sixty degrees around the room to address everyone, bowed, and smiled, causing the room to erupt in raucous cheers and whistles. The background music became louder, with the horns bellowing out shrill notes and drums beating faster and louder.

Mary, a wide, animated smile on her face, clapped with gusto. "He looks adorable," she said above the noise. "Everyone just loves him!"

Jason accepted the accolades, took the microphone from the stand, and leaned against the stool. The lights in the room dimmed except for the spotlight descending on him, like the heavens had opened up. He closed his eyes and sang a few measures of a soulful, throbbing song, when his foot slipped out of his shoe, causing him to lose his balance and push back on the stool. The stool slid out from underneath, and he fell to the floor with a crash. When the microphone hit his forehead, it sent an amplified boom throughout the room, followed closely by the screech of feedback and a gasp from the audience. And then silence.

Lindsey, her clapping hands paused in mid-air, gasped and looked at Mary.

"Oh, no!" Mary said, and the two women ran to Jason.

Lindsey dropped to the floor next to Jason, and Mary kneeled at his other side, grabbing his wrist to take his pulse. Lindsey gently pushed him flat on the floor as he attempted to sit up.

"Jason, can you hear me?" Lindsey asked. "Do you know where you are?"

His eyes were wide, and his face blushed pink. "I know where I wish I was," he said, covering his eyes with his hand. "In bed, so I could pull the blankets over my head and hide. Don't tell me that I just fell in front of my audience."

Lindsey sighed in relief. He couldn't be badly injured if he was able to joke. "How's your back? Anything hurt?"

"Back is fine. See." He rotated from side to side as Lindsey had made him do in the ER. "The only thing hurt is my pride." He locked Lindsey's gaze and twisted his mouth. "Even your magic hands can't fix that."

"Pulse is normal, Doctor," Mary said. She placed her hand on Jason's forehead. "Temp appears normal too."

"You're a doctor?" A man who had gathered with the crowd asked Lindsey.

"Yes," she replied, examining Jason's neck for any signs of sprains. "I'm *his* doctor." She looked at Jason and smiled, eliciting a wide grin from him.

A red knot had formed on Jason's forehead from the

smack of the microphone. Lindsey touched it, and he flinched. "Sore?"

"A little tender, that's all."

"I'll get some ice," Mary said, scurrying off to the kitchen.

"Isn't that one of your songs?" Lindsey pulled down Jason's bottom eyelids to check his eyes. She raised a finger, and he followed its movement with his eyes. " 'A Little Tender'?"

Jason chuckled. "You mean 'Love Me Tender'?"

She laughed at her confusion. "Close but no cigar."

He reached for her wrist. "That song reminds me of someone with a soft touch and a caring heart."

She broke her eye contact with him. "Let's see if we can get you to sit up." She helped him to a sitting position, while she asked the small crowd that had gathered to disperse and give him some air. She studied his reaction with her trained eye. "Feel dizzy or nauseous?"

"Really, I'm fine."

Mary returned with a plastic bag of ice and positioned it on Jason's forehead. "So what happened? How did you end up on your keester?" She held the ice to his head.

He rolled his eyes upward. "I didn't have my shoe on all the way because of the bandage on my broken toe. My foot slipped out, and I toppled backward."

"You should have kept on the sneakers like your doctor told you," Lindsey said, arching her eyebrow.

"Elvis can't wear white sneakers with a black leather outfit," Jason retorted.

"Yeah, Lind. What were you thinking?" Mary chimed in, a mischicvous smile covering her face.

Lindsey shook her head. "Well, Elvis is lucky he didn't end up with more than a little bump on the head."

"So am I okay? Can I finish my show?"

"Yes and no," Lindsey replied. "Your head seems fine, but I'm afraid the show is over for tonight. Where's Bernie? He needs to drive you home and sit with you for a couple of hours, just to make sure."

"Bernie's not here. Car trouble. Come on, Lindsey. I'm just fine. Let me finish singing," Jason pleaded. "What am I going to tell my audience?"

"How about, 'Elvis has left the building'?" Mary asked with a grin.

"They'll understand," Lindsey said. "Just blame it on your doctor." She patted his back.

Jason sighed and lowered his head.

"Now get up slowly. Mary, since you drove tonight, I'll drive Jason home in his car."

"Well didn't that work out just fine," Mary winked at her friend.

The two women helped Jason to his feet. He took a minute to center himself, waved to the cheering crowd, and then walked to the parking lot with Lindsey and Mary each holding an arm.

"Just doing my job," Lindsey said sternly to Mary.

"Of course, Doctor," Mary replied, as she poked her from behind.

Chapter Five

"You really didn't have to do this," Jason said as he unlocked the door to his apartment and entered with Lindsey close behind. "I was perfectly capable of finishing my show *and* driving myself home."

"Look, that microphone gave you a pretty good clunk on the noggin. You'll be fine, but you can't be too careful with hits to the head. No sense taking a chance and driving," Lindsey said, waving a finger at him. She held back from saying she'd never forgive herself if anything happened to him.

"Well, I'll say one thing," Jason said, turning on the light next to the couch. "I sure know how to pick a doctor!" He smiled and gestured for Lindsey to have a seat. "You take house calls to a whole new level."

"Part of the job. Uh, is there someone here who can keep an eye on you for a couple of hours?"

"Just me. Good thing, too, because this place is just about big enough for one person! A cozy fit for two."

Lindsey glanced around the tiny apartment. She'd driven by the old brick house countless times during her life and always noticed the lovely flower garden in the front yard and the many bird feeders that hung from the trees. She had no idea the building contained such a quaint little apartment. And she was oddly pleased to find out that Jason was the apartment's only inhabitant.

Although the apartment was small, the living room was nicely furnished and colorful. A multicolored, geometrically patterned area rug covered the hardwood floors and delineated a snug sitting area in front of the stone fireplace. Overstuffed plum-colored recliners and a couch gave the room a homey feel, and the eclectic paintings and sculptures on the walls hinted at Jason's varied tastes in artwork.

Lindsey found herself surprised that someone who wore outlandish costumes, gaudy tinted glasses, and glittery capes actually had such good taste in interior design. Just another hint, she hoped, that the Elvis thing really was a put-on and a minor aspect of this enigma called Jason Kincaid.

Jason appeared to have made good use of the space, displaying a few plants next to the window and a well-stocked bookshelf, scattered with various photographs, on the wall opposite the television. Except for the multitude of CDs overflowing from the CD rack onto the floor and the top of the stereo, everything was in order.

Despite the many eye-catching items, Lindsey noticed most the thing that was missing: Elvis memorabilia. Not a picture, not a statue, not a trace of The King.

"Can I get you something to drink?" asked Jason.

"No, thanks. Nice place."

"It's small but all I need since I'm usually alone anyway."

Usually alone? Does that mean there were times when he wasn't?

Jason kicked off the shoes that had led to his fall from grace and sat on the couch.

"Why don't you put that foot up?" Lindsey pointed to his bandaged toe. "Doesn't hurt to keep it elevated whenever you have a chance."

Jason lifted his legs onto the couch. "Doesn't seem like a very proper thing to do when I have a guest. So much for good manners."

"I'm your doctor, not a guest." She folded her hands on her lap and smiled demurely at him.

He nodded. "When I was flat on my back like some clumsy oaf, you were my doctor. But I'd like to think a lady in my apartment, even a lady who wields a mean stethoscope, is a guest." He cocked his head slightly and smiled.

Jason was much more charming and handsome than any celebrity he chose to mimic. Despite the outlandish costumes and on-stage persona, he was incredibly genuine and down to earth. Interestingly enough, the more Lindsey was with him, the less she noticed Elvis and the more she saw Jason, despite the costume.

"So who else lives in your building?" she asked.

"Miss Downing, the owner, lives downstairs on the left. She plants the garden and feeds all the birds in town. She's a sweet old lady with about a hundred cats that meow louder than a pack of wild tigers from all the birds she attracts. Ever notice old spinsters always seen to end up with a house full of cats?"

Lindsey shuddered. She hoped that in fifty years she wouldn't be like Miss Downing. Lily had already started the countdown. Just ninety-nine to go!

"Karen and Jack Lawson live in the apartment next to Miss Downing," Jason continued. He scratched his head and started to push off the wig.

Was he going to remove his wig?

Then he flicked his hand as if reconsidering and straightened the black matt on his head.

Disappointment washed over Lindsey as he continued to talk, wig still in place.

"They're newlyweds who teach at the high school," Jason said, expanding on his litany of tenants. "And this middle-aged woman, Eileen Peterson, lives in the apartment right across the hall. She runs the flower shop downtown."

"I know Eileen. She really does some nice arrangements."

"Well, you must keep her in business."

"I don't buy too many fresh arrangements," Lindsey said. "I have a lot of flowers in my yard."

Jason smiled. "I mean you must have a lot of flowers sent to you. You know, from admirers."

Lindsey felt her cheeks blush, and she lowered her eyes. "Only in my dreams." She realized the joke she hoped to make hadn't come off as she expected. Instead, she sounded pathetic. When she looked up, he was watching her, his expression a mix of genuine interest and playful doubt.

"Hmmm," he said. "A beautiful, talented, intelligent woman who is also modest. Rare find." He flashed her a wide smile that formed dimples in each cheek.

Was he flirting with her? Lindsey felt a strange sensation run from head to toe, and she was tempted to join him in a little spirited give-and-take. But doctors don't do that with their patients. Even if she wasn't technically on duty, and even if she was sitting in his apartment, she was still treating him for a bump to the head. So that meant she was working, not enjoying herself while she visited with an attractive man whose presence alone drummed up feelings that could propel her across the universe.

"So, how's the head feeling?" Lindsey, pleased for an excuse to change the subject, walked over to the couch to inspect the bump on Jason's forehead, touching it gingerly. "Swelling has gone down a little."

Jason reached up and placed his hand on hers, coaxing her to sit next to him on the couch.

"My head is fine," he said, his gaze locking hers. "I have the best doctor in town, remember?"

She wasn't sure if it was the soft slickness of his leather jacket on her bare arm or close proximity that caused her to shiver. She had been, after all, close to him when she examined him in the ER, but that was different. There she was doing her job. Here she was, well, she wasn't quite sure. Work had never felt like this.

"Cold?" Jason asked.

"Quite the opposite." Lindsey wished she could take back those words and hoped he hadn't caught the real meaning of her statement.

"You sure look pretty in pink," Jason said. "I was beginning to think all you ever wore was a white coat."

"That's my usual outfit." She pushed her hair behind her ears. Despite her head screaming to get up off the couch and remember her place with her patient, she wanted to stay put. Stay close. "I'll get some more ice," she said, finding it hard to tear her gaze from his.

"Kitchen is over there." Jason pointed to the left. "Plastic bags are on the counter."

Lindsey floated into the galley kitchen and filled a bag with ice. She returned to Jason, handed him the bag, and guided his frosty hand to his forehead. "Hold this for a while," she commanded gently.

"Why don't you flip on the stereo?" Jason scrunched his eyes. "This is the ultimate brain freeze."

Lindsey walked over to the stereo and pushed the CD button. "Let me guess whose music we'll hear."

"First time you've been wrong since I met you," he smiled.

Soft jazz sounds flowed through the apartment. Unsettled, rumbling notes collided with each other in the most unexpected way, scrambling so hard to come together, yet creating a most delightful tune when they did. Notes that were just sounds on their own but became music when they meshed. "I like it," Lindsey said, returning to the chair and reaching for her purse. "Will you excuse me while I call home?"

She pulled her cell phone from her purse and dialed, aware he was watching her, deliberately diverting her eyes from his. She was flattered, as well as flustered, by the attention and determined not to show it.

"Hi, Andrew," she said into her phone. "Look, I ran into a little . . . uh . . . emergency with a patient." She looked at Jason. "Can you stay with Grandpa? Is he asleep?"

Jason continued to look at her while she listened to the phone. He yawned, unzipped his leather jacket to reveal a red T-shirt that said NEW YORK STATE FAIR, and slipped lower onto the couch, still holding the ice bag on his head.

"Good, thanks," she said. "My cell is on if you need me." She flipped close the phone and put it back into her purse.

Jason yawned again.

"Tired?" Lindsey asked. "That painkiller I gave you can make you sleepy."

"That and I couldn't sleep last night because of this throbbing toe." Jason pointed to his foot. "And it's really a workout to perform—even half a show!"

Lindsey moved to the end of the couch and placed Jason's feet in her lap. "Let me rub your foot to help the soreness. You probably aggravated the toe again when you, uh, slipped." She proceeded to knead his foot between her fingers, being careful not to irritate the broken toe. "My patients tell me this really helps."

"You don't have to do that," Jason said, slipping lower into the couch. "You're my guest." He sighed, closed his eyes, and his face relaxed. "Ummm. That feels great."

"Thought I was your doctor," Lindsey volleyed. "You're going to have to make up your mind."

"My mind was made up long ago," he smiled, eyes still closed. "So who's Andrew?"

"The high school kid who lives next door. I don't like to leave Grandpa alone for too long, especially at night, so Andrew stays with him on those rare occasions I'm out or when I'm called into the hospital. He's a good kid."

"Good," Jason said, his voice sleepy as his head turned to the side.

"Good what?"

"Good he's not your boyfriend."

Jason's eyes closed tighter, and his breathing slowed. She continued to rub his foot and within a few minutes he was sound asleep. The ice bag fell off his head and onto the floor with a watery plop.

Lindsey gently moved his feet from her lap, stood,

and covered him with the afghan draped over the back of a chair. She picked up the melting bag of ice and deposited it in the kitchen sink.

On her way back to the recliner, she noticed the photographs scattered in frames on the bookshelves. One was of two young boys waving from the front of a tractor trailer cab. She recognized the older boy to be a young Jason. The smaller boy looked similar to him, but his eyes had a distant look and he wasn't focused on the camera.

Another photograph showed Jason and the other boy, a couple of years older, with a man who resembled them. The younger boy's gaze wandered from the camera, disconnected from the moment. Jason held the boy closely and smiled widely, his expression a mixture of pride and delight.

The last picture Lindsey noticed looked like a fairly recent shot of Jason with Niagara Falls in the background. He leaned against the railing, the great mist of the falls a cloud of glitter behind him. Those were the deep-brown eyes, dimpled cheeks, and square chin she'd come to recognize over the last couple of days. But the blond hair was something new to her. Without the Elvis topper, Jason had hair as blond as gold, making him look like he belonged on a beach, a tennis court, or a hiking trail—some outdoor destination that was as fresh and bright as he was. The wind blew his hair into careless, boyish wisps reflecting the sun. Her curiosity about the true Jason was satisfied, but her desire to see the real thing grew exponentially.

Lindsey took that picture and the one of Jason with the man and boy back to her chair and studied them under the light. She looked from the photographs to Jason sleeping on the couch, sizing him up. "Okay, so I've had a little glimpse into who you really are," she whispered to the still room. "You are quite the mystery, Jason Kincaid."

Lindsey yawned, stretched, and looked at her watch. Almost midnight. She had to get some sleep. At eight in the morning, another action-packed day in the ER would begin. She watched Jason's steady breathing and the peaceful expression on his face as he slept. He certainly seemed comfortable enough, and the redness of the bump was fading. It would probably be safe to leave him alone for the night. She could even stop by before work tomorrow. That would be in only about seven hours.

She started to get up from the chair but hesitated. There was always the outside chance the bruise would become painful during the night. Or he'd get up to use the bathroom, feel disoriented, and stumble again. If he were awake, she'd offer to take him back to her house and set him up in the guest room. But he was out like a light from the painkiller.

Well, he wouldn't be the first patient she spent the night caring for.

Lindsey replaced the photos on the bookshelf, took

her cell phone from her purse, walked into the kitchen, and called Andrew.

"Andrew, it's me again," she said when the teen answered the phone, sounding as if she woke him. She pictured him rolling off the couch in a daze when the phone rang. "Look, I have to stay with my patient all night. Sure you can stay with Grandpa?" She listened for his reply. "Make yourself at home in the guest room, and don't forget to lock the door. Thanks."

Lindsey settled back into the recliner, sinking low into the soft cushions. She slipped off her shoes and hiked up the footrest, stretching backward. The last thing she remembered was the comforting sound of Jason's breathing in rhythm with the tick of the second hand of the wall clock.

The birds at Miss Downing's feeders were chirping loudly in the breaking sun, causing Lindsey to jump upward with a start. She shook her head to orient herself; then the whole evening came back to her, reminding her why she'd spent the night curled like a pretzel in the recliner in Jason's apartment.

She glanced over to the couch. There was Jason, propped on his elbows, smiling, wig still in place and leather outfit apparently none the worse for the wear for having doubled as pajamas.

She looked at the clock, squinting to see it without her glasses. Seven-fifty. She was late for work! And Elvis was watching her!

Chapter Six

Lindsey hurried from the doctors' lounge, buttoning up her white coat, combing her fingers through her hair. She would have put on some lipstick, but she couldn't find her makeup kit, so she swished her tongue over her lips to moisten them. On the mad dash from Jason's apartment to the hospital, she called to check on Grandpa and the pets and verified that Andrew would be able to take care of everything until she was able to get home. She'd have to give him a big bonus for the extra help.

Lindsey zoomed up to the nurses' station in the ER, scurrying past a number of patients and enough activity to know the day already had "out of control" written all over it. She took a deep breath and stopped on a dime at the desk, revving up her energy to high gear. Mary smirked and handed her three charts.

"Hi, Mare." Lindsey took the charts and immediately perused the disasters awaiting her. "What do we have here?"

"Morning, Doctor," Mary said. "There's an infant with a rash in Exam Room Two, a boy with stomach pains in Three, and a pimple in Five."

"A pimple?" Lindsey scrunched up her face. "Are you serious?" Today was absolutely the wrong day for jokes.

"Well, to the teen queen of the Harbor Festival, a pimple is apparently a life or death situation. She has to have publicity photos taken today with her court, so she's freaking out about the headlight on her nose."

Lindsey shook her head and started to walk away. Just what she needed. "Thanks."

"Oh, Doctor," Mary called.

Lindsey turned back to her friend.

"Your pink dress hangs perfectly below your white coat."

Lindsey rolled her eyes upward and smirked.

"Uh, am I mistaken, or were you wearing pink last night when you drove Mr. Kincaid home?" Mary flashed an exaggerated wink.

Lindsey marched back to the desk and set down the charts with a thud. She leaned closely to her friend. "No wisecracks," she hissed quietly so no one would over-hear. "Jason fell asleep, and I stayed to keep an eye on him. That's it."

"Yes, Doctor. I do believe you."

"No, you don't!" Lindsey said, her voice getting louder

with emotion. "Shh!" She looked around. "What was I supposed to do? The guy had a bump on his head. I couldn't take the chance that he had a mild concussion."

"Whatever you say, Doctor," Mary continued, her mouth turning upward in a devilish grin.

"Stop with the doctor stuff," Lindsey commanded. "If I had a stupid alarm clock, I would have set it. I fell asleep in his chair and didn't have time to run home and change before work this morning."

"Certainly, Doctor," Mary said, her eyes bright with glee.

"Grrr," Lindsey growled as her frustration grew.

Mary gestured with her hands for Lindsey to calm down. "Look, Lind. I'm just teasing you. I know you'd do that for any of your patients. Hey, you stayed up all night with me when I had the flu last year. If you hadn't been late for work, I would have thought—hoped—that just maybe . . . But there's no way you'd be late for work because of some guy. I've seen you walk through a snow storm to get here. You're the most dedicated doctor I know. Even Elvis couldn't change that!"

Lindsey took a deep breath, stretched her neck, and rubbed her temples. "Sorry I overreacted. I'm just tired. I need a shower. And I need to get out of this dress."

"How is our star anyway?" Mary asked.

"Fine. He slept well, and the bump is healing nicely. The broken toe is better too."

Mary shook her head and chuckled. "He must be the klutziest Elvis in the history of the world."

"Tell me about it! I've got to look in on these patients. I don't want to keep little Miss Pimple Queen waiting!" Lindsey picked up the charts and started for the exam rooms.

"Hope this doesn't turn into a hard day's night," Mary said, her voice lilting.

Lindsey turned around and mouthed "what?" to Mary.

Mary broke out into a wide grin. "Oops. Wrong celebrity!"

Lindsey shook a scolding finger, turned on her heels, and tramped to her first patient.

"I'll put on some fresh coffee, Doctor," Mary called after her. "You're going to need it."

After convincing the festival queen the best remedy for her pimple was a dab of makeup, Lindsey took advantage of the lull in the action and hurried to the doctors' lounge to shower. She changed into the spare slacks, blouse, and underwear she always kept in her locker. Several times she'd had to change because someone bled on her or missed the bucket. Being an ER doctor taught her to be prepared for anything. Except for what to do when an incredibly cute, charming, and accident-prone Elvis impersonator kept stumbling into the hospital.

That was one lesson she'd have to figure out for herself.

At around eleven-thirty, Lindsey dashed home to check on her grandfather and the pets. Andrew was still there, and he and Tom were enjoying some burgers and fries from the fast-food restaurant. She cringed when the greasy smell hit her as she walked in the door. Tom loved junk food, and Lindsey rarely let him have it. But considering the circumstances, she wouldn't complain. Andrew had been a real lifesaver, and she sure couldn't expect the kid to cook healthy meals too.

When she was assured everything at home was in order and Tom had his medication, Lindsey grabbed a few fries from Tom's plate, kissed him, hugged Andrew, stroked the pets, and dashed back to the ER, arriving a few minutes before noon and just in time for the committee meeting in the cafeteria.

She bought a salad and an orange juice, charged it to the tab she'd set up, and joined the other committee members who were already eating at a table by the large picture window.

"Hi, everyone. Sorry I'm late." She set her tray at the table and slid into a seat.

"We know how busy you've been with some patients," said Mary, arching her eyebrows at her friend.

"And I do appreciate your understanding," Lindsey shot back, plastering a rigid smile on her face.

While the committee ate, they chatted about the wonderful weather the region had been having, passed pleasantries about each others' families, and laughed about Henry's suggestion to change the hospital gowns to a calypso-orange pattern to brighten up the place.

As Lindsey stuffed the last bite of her salad into her mouth, she opened her notebook and started the meeting.

"As you all know, we need to raise some serious money for the care center or else the board of directors may put a stop to our plans."

"They give too much power to those people," Enrique said in his heavy Spanish accent, raising a finger to emphasize his point. The sunlight through the window reflected on the fringe of steely gray hair circling his bald crown. "The good people of Owl Cove need this center. I hope to one day bring over my mother from Madrid, and it is there she will live."

"I like your spirit," Lindsey said to him. "We need that commitment—and a lot of money—to give this project the real push it needs."

"Lind, what about that clam bake you suggested?" asked Mary. She opened a package of peanut butter cookies, took one, and passed the box around the table.

"What does everyone else think?" asked Lindsey. "Clam bakes usually get a good turnout. Everyone loves sitting on the lakeshore and eating good food."

"It is a very good idea," said Sanjay, his slight Indian accent a clue to the many years that he's lived in America. "We could hold it at the picnic ground by the lake, where the hospital has its summer volunteer party. It accommodates many people." As he spoke, he wrote in a notebook, then hesitated while he took a small calculator from his pocket and punched some buttons.

"The cost per person would be about ten dollars," Sanjay continued, "assuming the fish market gives us a good deal. If we sell tickets for twenty dollars, which is a reasonable price, we can get back our costs plus make a good profit."

"Good idea," Julie said. She took three cookies from the box Mary passed around and munched on them, momentarily satisfying the bottomless pit that was a sharp contrast to her almost skeletal physique.

"At the last clam bake, the hospital made five thousand dollars." Sanjay flipped to another page in his notebook to report that result. "That was very good, very good indeed. People around here certainly love their clams!"

"And I can play my guitar to entertain the guests!" said Enrique.

"And then Lindsey can treat them for earaches!" Julie joked, eliciting laughs from everyone, including Enrique.

Lindsey chewed on her pen. "If we could bring in five thousand dollars, that would be a good start. But we need to do more than that."

"How about a holiday craft show," suggested Mary. "We could have it in September at the start of the fall-winter holiday season. Owl Cove has a lot of crafty people who may like to participate. I see a lot of hand-made goods in the gift shops in town. We can ask those shopkeepers who they buy from and solicit those people."

Sanjay flipped to another page in his notebook. "My son's hockey team held a craft show last year and charged each crafter fifty dollars to rent a table. They also charged a modest admission price of five dollars per person. Those charges, coupled with the income from the baked goods they sold, helped raise three thousand dollars."

"I'm sure a lot of the women who knit the baby bonnets and booties for the preemies would like to participate," said Julie, wiping some cookie crumbs from her mouth.

"These are wonderful ideas, and I think we should pursue them, but we need one really big hit that will bring in a small windfall," Lindsey said, making a fist.

"How much time do we have?" Enrique asked.

"According to Henry, not much," Lindsey replied. "The board wants to know financing for the final plans is in place so they can break ground by early spring . . . or not at all."

"Uh, Lind," Mary said, clearing her throat. She stiffened and looked over Lindsey's head. "I think someone is here to see you." She pointed a finger behind her friend.

When Lindsey turned around, her face was just a nose away from a large bouquet of white daisies wrapped in green tissue paper and tied with an enormous red bow. Startled, she slowly raised her eyes upward over the flowers.

There was the smiling face of Jason—as Elvis. His yellow jumpsuit, complete with a stand-up collar, studded butterfly design that filled the entire front, and short cape that hung off one shoulder made him hard to miss in the white-coat world of the cafeteria. Bernie stood next to him, smiling widely and looking from Jason to Lindsey and back again.

"Just a small thank you for all the care you've given me lately, Lindsey." Jason handed her the flowers.

"They're beautiful!" Lindsey exclaimed. "How lovely!" All eyes in the cafeteria were on Jason and the impromptu celebrity sighting everyone was enjoying with their lunches. Lindsey hadn't seen such a stir since Halloween when Henry, dressed like Dracula, handed out chocolate pumpkins to all the diners.

"You can thank Eileen for that," Jason said. "She fixed this up especially for you at her flowershop."

Lindsey blushed when she flashed back to the comment Jason made last night about all the flowers Lindsey must get. If only he knew these were the first ones she'd received since . . . she couldn't even recall.

Lindsey stood and zeroed in on the small bruise on Jason's forehead, a souvenir from last night's fiasco. She touched it gently. "Swelling is gone. Feel okay?"

"Never better," Jason replied, his mouth turning into a half-grin.

"How's the toe?" She looked down to see yellow boots that matched his costume.

"Left the sneakers at home today." He moved his foot back and forth. "My feet feel like they've been magically rubbed into perfect condition!"

Lindsey caught the twinkle in his eye and his offhanded reference to last night's foot massage.

"The back?" she asked, continuing with the grocery list of maladies.

He did a few Elvis trademark twists and turns, which caused scattered claps throughout the cafeteria. "You be the judge," he said, again flashing her a smile. "I'd say The King is back in business."

Lindsey couldn't contain her smile. "Just don't overdo it, King," she said with light sarcasm. "You're starting to run out of body parts!"

"Doc, you've been mighty kind to this boy," Bernie commented. "We look forward to the chance to repay the favor. The flowers are just a small token."

"You really didn't have to," Lindsey began, taking another whiff of the daisies, closing her eyes to enjoy a momentary respite. They smelled fresh and grassy and clean.

"You deserve much more," Jason said, his eyes still fixed on her.

"Just doing my job."

"Sorry to interrupt your meeting," Jason said, glancing toward the table. "I can see you're all busy. We're on our way to do an ... an appearance at St. John's Nursing Home, so we won't keep you any longer."

Lindsey took a deep breath. So that explained the costume in the middle of the day. Thank goodness.

As the men headed out the door, the cafeteria broke into applause, causing Jason to turn and wave to the crowded room as if he were exiting a show. A few people in the corner started singing "Shake, Rattle, and Roll" and doing a few dance moves.

Lindsey really didn't get it, but one thing was certain: people loved the whole Elvis aura. The songs, the moves, and the fun have endured long after the real Elvis departed. Perhaps she was missing something. One thing was certain; with Jason involved, her curiosity was certainly piqued.

"Well, someone is quite the popular doctor," Mary said. "Just look at those flowers!" She threw her friend a coquettish grin as Lindsey sat down with the bouquet overflowing in her lap.

"They are bigger than the bushes in front of the hospital," Sanjay grinned.

"He is a very thoughtful gentleman," said Enrique.

Julie's eyes were open wide and her face was blank. "Only Elvis could put on such a show by just delivering flowers!" She looked stunned, like she'd just seen a vision or won an enormous prize. Suddenly, she pounded the table with her fist then clapped excitedly. "That's it! That's our big money maker!"

"A flower sale?" asked Sanjay.

"No, no," said Julie, catching her breath as she hurried to speak. "We'll hire Jason to put on his Elvis show!"

"Now you're talking!" Mary chimed in. "You heard how everyone cheered at just the sight of him."

"Perhaps he would need a guitar accompaniment," Enrique added.

"No," the rest of the committee again said as a chorus.

"What do you think, Lind?" asked Mary, rubbing her hands together. "Great idea or what? You saw what a great show he put on at the Harbor Grill."

"I . . . I guess that would be a . . . a good idea," Lindsey said with hesitation. Actually, it was the best fundraising idea the committee had. Yet the thought of asking Jason to perform struck a sour note. He was the one she was interested in, not Elvis. She just wasn't having any luck separating the two.

"He may be booked up," Lindsey said, excuses scrambling in her head. "Sounds like he does a lot of shows."

"We will not know unless we ask," said Sanjay.

"I don't know what he charges," Lindsey added. "May be too expensive for our budget."

"We must spend money to make money," Sanjay added.

"Who votes that we check out an Elvis show?" asked Julie, raising her hand and waving it with a wild enthusiasm.

Mary, Sanjay, and Enrique quickly thrust their hands into the air.

Lindsey looked around the table at the sea of waving hands and slowly raised hers. What else could she do? From a fundraising viewpoint, this was the perfect solution. From a personal viewpoint, she had her doubts. She inhaled and tried to put the situation in perspective. The last thing she would do was let her feelings stand in the way of the care center. She certainly didn't want to contradict the committee and cause anyone to get the wrong idea about Jason and her. Oh no. If anyone thought she had any interest in Jason other than as a patient, why, she'd . . . she'd . . . Her mind went blank. What would she do?

"Let us know what he says after you talk to him," Julie said, as the committee members stood to leave. "Since you two are on a first-name basis, you probably won't mind asking."

"Why do I—," Lindsey began. Before she had a chance to finish, the rest of the committee was chatting excitedly about their plans and walking out the door. Lindsey was alone at the table, hidden behind the flowers.

"Oh, meeting adjourned," she said, slamming shut her notebook.

Chapter Seven

Jason, decked out in his red Elvis costume, Bernie at his side, approached the nurses' station in the ER. They stood quietly until Mary looked up from the chart she was writing on.

Her eyes opened wide. "Not again."

"And hello to you, too, Mary," Jason said, a touch of sarcasm in his voice.

"Ma'am," Bernie added with a bow of his head.

Mary furrowed her brow, leaned over the desk, and took a sweep of Jason from head to toe. "Nothing broken or bleeding. Anything going on under that red suit I need to know about? Pains, strains?"

"No repairs needed this time," Jason laughed.

"Whew!" Mary replied with an exaggerated wipe of

her hand across her forehead. "You had me worried for a minute."

"He has been your best customer recently, hasn't he?" Bernie chuckled.

"Not that we don't like to see you, Jason, but seeing you all in one piece is preferred." Mary smiled widely. "Like yesterday, when you came to give Lindsey those flowers."

"I prefer it that way too!" Jason replied. "I don't have any flowers today, but this is a social call. Is Lindsey here?"

"She's with a patient. You can wait over there if you want to." Mary pointed to a small waiting room. "She won't be long."

The two men took a seat in the waiting room that was occupied by a handful of other people. Jason smiled at those who glanced curiously at him, waved hello, and shouted "Hey, Elvis."

"Cool outfit, dude," said a teenager with heavily tattooed arms and spiked hair.

"It was in 1965," Jason replied. He was used to all types of comments. Most were complimentary or remarks made in good fun. Once in a while, he was heckled or insulted. Regardless, he took each comment, good or bad, for what it was: someone's words, nothing more. His childhood had taught him to not place much importance on what others said. He knew how cruel some comments could be, how hurtful. His father had instilled in him the idea that it was always best to be yourself and not pass judgment. Everyone had some heartache deep down inside.

"Are you the real Elvis come back from the grave?" asked a middle-aged woman in a Grateful Dead T-shirt, who studied Jason through thick glasses.

"Afraid not," Jason chuckled.

"Sure? There's a strong resemblance if you ask me. I've heard those stories speculating on whether Elvis really died."

"Thanks for the compliment, ma'am, but I'm just having some fun."

The woman, who returned to the magazine she was reading, lifted her eyes every few minutes to check out Jason, as if she were trying to catch him incarnate into the real thing.

A man who appeared to be in his late seventies watched Jason intently. A look of contentment washed over the man's face, then he closed his eyes and smiled, as if he'd been taken to a peaceful place. After a few minutes, he left his chair at the far end of the room and hobbled over with his cane to the empty chair next to Jason.

"Hello, friend," Jason said to the man who leaned closely to him.

"I know you're just a performer, not the real thing," the man said, tightly clutching a straw hat. "But I just have to tell you something. Many, many years ago, before we were married, I took my late wife to an Elvis concert." The man lifted his eyes and his expression took on that warm, thoughtful serenity of someone enjoying a precious memory. "Elvis was just starting out then, and he put on one heck of a show. Helen and I had such a grand time laughing, singing, and cheering. I can still see the ecstatic look on her face and the way that ribbon she wore in her hair flopped up and down as she jumped in her seat." He chuckled softly.

"Must have been some show," Jason said.

"Oh, it was. It certainly was," the man said, his voice drifting. "Helen was so excited. Halfway through the show, she grabbed my hand and looked me square in the eyes. 'Carl,' she said. 'Let's always be as happy as we are at this moment.'" The man wiped a tiny tear from the corner of his eye and took a minute to compose himself. "And we were. We made it a point to always be that happy. Let me just thank you, young man, for making that memory come alive for me one more time. Today is a difficult day. I'm afraid because my sister was rushed here a couple of hours ago. And, well, we're not sure what's wrong. So this little piece of joy you brought me has meant so much."

"That's a beautiful story," Jason said, his throat tightening with emotion.

The man reached over and clasped Jason's hand. "You gave an old man a reason to smile today."

After the man returned to his seat, Jason turned to Bernie. "He gave me a reason to smile for a lifetime. There's something to be said for good memories."

"We all have our fair share, son," Bernie replied.

"And there are plenty more to be made. If we just do the right things, we'll have more good memories than we'll know what to do with."

"I'm with you on that one." Jason clasped Lindsey's makeup kit in his hands.

"Say, did you notice those little posters on the wall askin' for donations to some new long-term and geriatric care center the hospital is fixin' to build?" Bernie pointed to the wall across from where they sat. "I see the Doc's name is listed as the contact. Now doesn't that sound like a good cause for the fine folks in this town? Figures a kind woman like the Doc is in charge of this."

Jason studied the poster. "Hmm. Wish I could help out. Sounds like a place that's similar to St. John's Nursing Home. With all the talk of St. John's closing in a couple of years, I'd sure like to know the care center was available, you know, in case we need it."

Bernie rested his chin in his hands and pursed his lips. "Maybe there is a way we can help," he said, his tone thoughtful.

"How? They'll need more than the couple hundred dollar donation I could afford to give."

Bernie thought for a few moments. "Well, you've been wishin' for a way to show the good doctor how much you appreciate her care. And I've been tryin' to find new gigs for you, keep growin' that followin'. What if we combine the two and do a free show to benefit the care center? That could help the townfolks, and it might just make the Doc take notice, if you know what I mean." Bernie grinned and elbowed Jason. "She sure is a pretty one."

"I'm all for doing a benefit, but I don't think she'll go for it," Jason said. "I get the feeling Lindsey thinks my Elvis career is, how shall I say it, a little wacky." He laughed, primped his wide collar, and adjusted the enormous cufflinks. "What do you think gave her that idea?" he asked.

Bernie laughed. "Well, this is a far cry from your old job as a CPA!"

"So I traded in my shirt and tie for a cape and boots." He gestured to his clothing. "One monkey suit for another."

"You're some fancy-dressin' monkey!" Bernie laughed a little too loudly for the quiet waiting room, causing some people to look his way and prompting a toddler to point at Jason.

"I'd just like to do something special for Lindsey," Jason began. "Show her that under the crazy costume, there's someone who'd like to get to know her better. Know if—"

"Let me handle it," Bernie interrupted, gesturing like he had it all under control. "That's what a manager is for."

Lindsey wrote notes on the chart as she hurried out of the exam room. At the nurses' station, she placed the chart into Mary's open hand. "What a cute baby! Even with a hundred and three temp, she smiled like a little trooper. Wish all my patients were so easy."

"I just wish they were all real," Mary giggled.

"Huh?" Lindsey shook her head, not quite comprehending Mary's comment. "Okay, who's our next guest on the party list?"

"In there." Mary gestured with a nod of her head to the waiting room.

Lindsey pulled her glasses out of the breast pocket of her white coat and plopped them on her nose. Through the door of the waiting room, she saw Jason and Bernie. She did a double-take and snapped her head back to Mary.

"He's baaaack," Mary sang out. "And looking mighty cute if you ask me."

"Don't tell me he hurt something else," Lindsey said, raising her hands to her head. "And again with the garb!" What she wouldn't give to see Jason dressed as himself and at a location other than the hospital.

"He said it's a social call," Mary replied. "Not even a paper cut that needs your doctoring today!"

Lindsey huffed. "Social call? What is that supposed to mean?"

Mary nodded. "Apparently, our hospital is also a dating service."

"Dating service? He doesn't have more flowers, does he?" Lindsey again turned to look in the waiting room. She didn't see any flowers, but she noticed Jason's well-sculpted profile and broad shoulders. What height had his chart indicated? Six-one? Somewhere close to perfect.

"No, but he had some little purse in his hands. Just go find out what he wants. Thought you'd be happy to see him."

Lindsey wrinkled her nose. "I am, but . . . here? There's always such a fuss when he shows up. I need to concentrate on my work. And that's hard to do when I'm so . . . distracted." She was whining, but once the words started, they took on a life of their own.

"Well, he's someone special. Think about it. How many men are two great guys rolled into one?"

Lindsey furrowed her brow into a V. "Two great guys?"

"Jason and Elvis." Mary gestured with outstretched palms.

"Not you, too, Mare," Lindsey moaned. "Enough with the Elvis thing. I mean, the guy was history even before we were born. Yeah, maybe he was some superstar from days gone by, but Jason is not him. Jason pretends to be him. That's all. *Pretends.*" Lindsey bit her lip. "And that's weird enough."

"I think it's pretty cool. Just see what he wants. Now may be a good chance to ask him to do a benefit for the care center."

Lindsey rubbed a kink in her neck. "I don't think so," she said, keeping one eye on Jason.

Mary motioned with her hands for Lindsey to talk. "Okay, what's going on? This is me you're talking to. Out with it."

Lindsey drew closer to her friend. She removed her glasses and pushed her hair behind her ears. Then she adjusted the stethoscope around her neck and took a deep breath. "I really like Jason. I mean, beyond thinking he's just a nice guy who's incredibly clumsy. I'd like to get to know him, not Elvis, better. Right now, the two are so intertwined it's hard to tell the difference. Wouldn't asking him to do a show be like throwing gasoline on the fire?" Lindsey looked at Mary with pleading eyes.

"Would that be so bad?" Mary touched Lindsey's arm. "How about if you just learn to relax a little and take things as they come? If Jason really turns out to be that someone special, will the stupid wig and goofy costumes really matter? Who knows, if you give it a chance, you may just become an Elvis fan, as well as a Jason fan."

Lindsey inhaled deeply as Mary's words sank in. What choice did she really have? She could forget Jason ever walked into—or, rather, was carried into—the ER. That would mean forgetting about his gentle demeanor, dazzling personality, sweet smile, and perfect physique. Or she could learn to accept Elvis. Lindsey shuddered and headed to the waiting room.

"Well, this is a surprise," she said, walking up to Jason and Bernie, wondering how convincing she could sound to make them believe this was the first moment she saw them. She'd never admit she'd been watching them for the last ten minutes trying to build up her nerve.

They stood to greet her.

"Now admit it, Lindsey. Are you really surprised to

see us, or are you just surprised to see me in one piece?"
Jason cocked his head and smiled, accentuating his
dimple.

"Both," Lindsey smiled broadly. So all it took was
one charming comment from this guy to make her forget why she wanted to avoid him. "Actually, I'm glad
you're here. I was going to call you today and thank you
for the flowers. You should see how pretty they look on
the living room table."

"I'd like to see that," Jason said decisively.

"Oh, sure, anytime," Lindsey said, unable to take back
the comment-turned-invitation. She wasn't displeased
Jason had responded so well.

"Just say when," Jason continued like a bulldog who
wasn't about to back down.

Bernie glanced at him from the corner of his eye and
nodded slowly, holding back a chuckle.

"Oh, well, uh . . . ," Lindsey stuttered. "Well, how
about tomorrow for dinner? I'll put some chicken and
steaks on the grill."

"Great. Just give me the address and I'll be there."
Jason's eyes didn't veer from hers.

Lindsey took out her prescription pad and scribbled
down her address and phone number. Was there really a
man standing in front of her who looked like Elvis?
And was she really giving him directions to her house?

"Bernie, the invitation is for you too," Lindsey said.
"Grandpa will certainly enjoy seeing both of you again."

"I'd be honored, Doc," Bernie said with a bow of

head. "Nothing like a nice grilled steak to put a smile on a man's face."

"Oh, I almost forgot why we stopped by," Jason said, dangling Lindsey's makeup kit in front of her. "I found this on the floor next to the recliner. You must have dropped it the other night."

Lindsey noticed the lift of the eyebrows on the woman sitting close to her. She sighed as she imagined herself becoming the next topic of juicy gossip: Lindsey Bartlett, doctor to the fake stars!

"Oh, there it is." She took the small purse from Jason, feeling a little spark when their fingers touched. "I've torn apart my car and house looking for this! You didn't have to make a special trip to return it."

"Just on our way to make a little appearance at a fiftieth anniversary party. No problem at all to stop by. Thought you may be missing your makeup kit, even though you sure don't need it," Jason smiled.

Lindsey shifted her stance. "If I didn't have something to cover up these tired circles, I'd scare a lot of patients!" She joked to divert the compliments she'd never been able to accept easily. She remembered her grandfather telling her when she was a child that some day a boy was sure to pay her a compliment. She should always keep in mind a truly pretty woman didn't know quite how pretty she was.

"Say, Doc," Bernie began. He pointed to the poster on the wall. "Think you could ever use help from us to raise some money for that new care center? An Elvis show?"

Lindsey caught her breath. While she was standing here talking, she was mulling in her head how she would ever ask Jason to do the show. Still not convinced it was the right move, for her anyway, she hadn't been able to squeeze out the words. And now Bernie had saved her the trouble.

"Well, yeah, maybe," she said, still unsettled by the coincidence of Bernie's offer.

"We'd like to help," Jason added.

Lindsey smiled. "Actually, the committee tossed around the idea. But we don't have a very big budget to work with and . . ."

Bernie held up his hand to quiet her. "Here's our offer," he began. "The price is free, and Jason will perform whenever and wherever you'd like. Give it some thought, and we can talk more at your place tomorrow."

"That's way too generous an offer," Lindsey replied. "I . . . I don't know if we'd ever be able to repay you."

"You already have," Jason said, reaching for her hand.

Chapter Eight

Lindsey rushed into the house, her arms filled with grocery bags and her head filled with apprehension about dinner. In between patients, she had agonized over what to serve for dinner with a greater intensity than she agonized over what medication to prescribe to her patients. At least with medication, she was confident she'd make the right choice. Dinner guests, especially ones who had made her question everything she thought she knew about herself, were few and far between at her home.

She wasn't sure what side dishes would go well with the grilled steak and chicken, how much lemonade to make, and what conversation could possibly take place. She flip-flopped between thinking the dinner would be a fun event to being convinced it would be nothing less than a national disaster. Her plan to hurry to the grocery store after work and then go home and bake a cake so the house would be filled with the sweet, comforting aroma of fresh baked goods hit the skids when the Benson twins showed up fifteen minutes before her shift was to end with sprained ankles from hanging on their playsets. If bad things came in threes, that meant one train wreck was still left to happen.

When she finally left the hospital, Lindsey drove a little too quickly to the store. There, she cruised hastily up and down the aisles, filling the cart with the necessities for dinner and a few extra desserts since, thanks to the twins, she wouldn't have time to bake. She kept glancing at her watch as she impatiently waited in the checkout line, loaded the bags into the back seat of the car, and was stuck behind every slow driver in town. This was a sign, she told herself, that she was meant to be a doctor, not host dinner parties for pretend celebrities.

She stopped abruptly in front of Tom, who was sitting on the couch. "Grandpa, why are you in your pajamas? Don't you feel well?"

"Fit as a fiddle." He craned his neck around her to see the television.

"Why are you dressed for bed? It's only five-thirty."

He looked at the clock hanging over the television. "Well, I'll be. Last time I looked, I thought it said eight-thirty. These old peepers must be playing tricks on me!"

"Well, why don't you get changed for dinner."

Tom rubbed his chin while he thought. "I'll just keep

my pajamas on. In just a few hours, it will be time for bed anyway."

She sighed. "But we're having guests for dinner, re-member? Jason and Bernie."

His bushy eyebrows wrinkled as he thought. "Reckon I do remember you saying something about that this morning." He hoisted himself from the chair with a grunt, grabbed his cane, and wobbled into the bedroom. "It's not like they never saw a man in his nightclothes," Tom mumbled.

"Hmm," said Lindsey to the empty room, as she sprinted to the kitchen and unpacked the bags. Tom seemed to be more forgetful each day. Lately, she'd felt anxious about what she might find when she came home from work. Thank goodness there hadn't been any dis-asters yet and she had Andrew to look in on Tom. For now, anyway.

After the groceries were put away, Lindsey washed the few dishes in the sink and cleaned up a spill of milk Tom must have made. "No big deal," she said softly, as she wiped the floor, feeling her anxiety rising. "It's just milk. I'm surprised Jingle and Lily didn't beat me to it."

When the groceries were put away and the kitchen was in order, she reached into the cupboard for two cans of pet food. As she scraped the food from the cans into their bowls, she called for Jingle and Lily, as she always did. Usually, their sixth sense and hungry tum-mies had them waiting at their empty bowls before Lindsey even arrived home from work.

When neither came running, she called them again. "Lily. Jingle. Dinner." She listened for the sound of scrambling toenails on the linoleum. Nothing.

"Where are the animals?" Lindsey asked Tom, who was exiting his bedroom, properly dressed except for the shirt that was buttoned wrong.

"Good question." Tom plopped in his chair. "Seems they were here earlier."

Lindsey inhaled quickly as her panic rose. She took a quick spin around the rest of the house, looking for a sign of her beloved pets. Then she hurried to the back door off the kitchen. Her heartbeat stepped up a bit when she found the door open a crack. Looking into the backyard, she saw the dog sitting on the chaise, basking in the late day sun. "Get in here, Jingle. How did you get out there?"

The greyhound perked up at the sound of his name and the sight of his mistress and ran for the door. He charged past her to the food bowl and started to wolf down his dinner.

Lindsey went into the yard to look for a sign of the other AWOL pet. "Lily? Lily, where are you? Where's my good girl?" She looked under the picnic table, in the garden, and in the shed, the usual places Lily hid during her outdoor escapades. No sign of the crafty feline.

As the fear of any danger her cat may be in started to mix with the panic of running behind schedule for dinner, Lindsey heard a little meow from above. She looked up and there was Lily, lounging lazily on the large vertical branch of the maple tree. "Don't tell me you're up there again. Lily, come down here. Be my good girl." She reached up, but the cat turned away, rubbing her head on the branch and purring so loudly Lindsey heard her from the ground.

"Lily, come on. I don't have time to play now."

The cat ignored her, seeming to purposely turn her head away.

With her hands on her hips, Lindsey looked upward and scolded the cat. "Okay, missy. I want you down here *right now.*"

Lily flapped her tail defiantly and twisted like a snake, scratching her back on the rough bark of the tree, flaunting her independence.

"Now I'm mad," Lindsey said, storming back into the house, the screen door flapping behind her. She didn't have time to get out the ladder and drag Lily out of the tree, as she'd done many times before. The stubborn cat would come down when she was hungry or decided she wanted to be rubbed.

"Grandpa, you have to remember to keep the back door closed," Lindsey called to Tom, raising her voice so he could hear her over the television. She pulled out the dishes and silverware for dinner, setting them on the counter with a clank, and arranged four tall lemonade glasses on a tray.

"Say something?" Tom called back to her.

"The door, Grandpa. Remember to keep the back

door closed so the animals don't get out. That TV is so loud." She grimaced with impatience.

"I did close it." He flipped through the channels with the remote control.

"Well, it was open." She pulled a clean tablecloth and napkins from the linen cupboard and closed the door with a backwards push of her behind.

"That darn cat jumps up and hits the handle to let herself out. Saw it with my own eyes."

The same eyes that thought the clock said eight-thirty instead of five-thirty. Whatever. She didn't have time to worry about that now.

When everything in the kitchen was ready, or at least as ready as it was going to be, Lindsey dashed upstairs to change. She took a quick shower and rinsed her hair, spritzing on some lilac body spray. As she was reapplying her makeup and brushing on some color to brighten up her fair complexion, she thought of Jason saying she didn't need makeup. She decided he was just being polite and gave herself an extra swish of blush.

Standing before her open closet, she pulled out three outfits. She rejected the pink sundress and tossed it on the bed. Jason had already seen that at his show the other night. She held up green capri pants and a navy blue sundress in front of the cheval mirror, alternating them and tilting her head to get an idea of how they may look. She liked how the green capris made her eyes stand out, but she decided on the blue sundress and threw the pants on the bed. She'd clean up later.

Lindsey wiggled into her dress, ran her fingers through her wet hair, hung a string of blue and white beads around her neck, and started downstairs. Bare feet! She ran back to the closet and slipped into a pair of navy slides.

Back in the kitchen, she took the rolls from the bakery bag and arranged them in the breadbasket before covering them with a cloth. She wiped up some water Jingle had splattered from her bowl and threw a pile of junk mail that had been collecting on the counter into the drawer.

The doorbell rang, and Lindsey fought the impulse to hurry to the door. She took a deep breath to compose herself and walked calmly.

"You expecting someone?" Tom asked. He put the last bite of a candy bar into his mouth.

"You're eating candy?"

Tom looked at the empty wrapper in his hand. "Guess I am."

"But we haven't eaten dinner yet!" She reminded herself that if Tom was too full for dinner at least he wouldn't eat the entire salad as he did last month before Mary came over. When Lindsey had reached into the refrigerator for the salad bowl, all that remained were a couple slips of carrot and a green olive.

Lindsey shook her head to brush off her aggravation with her grandfather, gave a quick fluff of her still-damp hair, rehearsed a sophisticated smile, and opened the door.

Her eyes bounced from Elvis to Bernie and back to Elvis. She hoped the expression on her face didn't match her dismay. She was expecting Jason, not Elvis, although, technically she had invited Elvis. But not really. Regardless, Elvis showed up.

Lindsey wanted to see the blond guy from the photo, not the incarnation of a ghost who was becoming all too familiar to her. She forced a smile and looked from Jason/Elvis to Bernie. Thank goodness Bernie was just Bernie.

"Come in; come in." She stepped aside to welcome the men into the living room.

"You look great," Jason said, handing her a bottle of wine.

"Why thank you." She wished she could say the same about him. He was wearing a kelly green jumpsuit she hadn't seen before, and she was relieved she'd rejected her own green pants and the opportunity to turn into his bookend.

"We appreciate your hospitality, Doc," Bernie said, placing a box of chocolates topped with a large white bow in her hands.

"Totally my pleasure." She propped open the outside door so that a fresh, soft breeze trickled through the screen door.

"Hope we're not late," Jason said. "I had another appearance at St. John's. I didn't want to waste time by running home and changing."

Lindsey wanted to say she would have gladly waited

for him to transform into a real person. Into the person who made her smile and question everything she thought she knew about herself. She would have been thrilled to hold up dinner for a while if she could see the real Jason. On the other hand, she appreciated his eagerness to see her. She couldn't fret about this now. She had a dinner party to run.

"Grandpa, you remember Jason and Bernie?"

Tom's face lit up when he recognized them, and he raised his finger in the air. "The young fellas from the festival. Lindsey, you should have told me they were coming."

"Must have slipped my mind, Grandpa," she said, punctuating her statement with a lift of her eyebrows.

"Nothing like a little surprise to get things rolling," Jason said, spiking the atmosphere with some levity.

"So, what do you think?" Lindsey gestured with a sweep of her hands to the vase of daisies on the table. "Told you they look beautiful."

"Whoo-eee. Pretty as a picture, just like the lady of the house," Bernie said.

"Eileen is some florist," Jason said. "I imagine you haven't seen the last of her arrangements." He winked.

Lindsey felt her stomach do a few flutters, and she wasn't sure why. Perhaps it was from hearing Jason's kind words, having him in her home, catching his subtle glimpses. Whatever the reason, she suddenly felt very happy about the prospect of enjoying a lovely evening with the two guests she'd invited—and the one she didn't.

"Let's go into the backyard and have a lemonade before I turn on the grill." She pointed to the back door and pulled Tom to his feet, then handed him his cane.

When everyone was settled outside, Lindsey served the lemonade with a small plate of assorted cheeses and crackers. The four chatted about the weather, listened to a few humorous stories about Jason's performances, and took a little tour around the yard to see the variety of roses in Lindsey's garden.

"That one is almost a perfect match for your hair," Jason commented, pointing to a pale tangerine rose. "May I?"

Lindsey nodded, and he plucked a blossom and placed it behind her ear. "The perfect spot for a beautiful flower."

The glow from Jason's compliment was quickly extinguished by Lindsey's thought that she'd never be able to find a flower to match his hair. *Get rid of the wig*, she wanted to shout.

While the men visited, Lindsey turned on the grill and ran back into the kitchen to toss the salad. She watched them through the open kitchen window.

"Right up there," Tom said, pointing at Lily sprawled out over the branch. "Darn thing has a mind of her own."

"There's no talkin' to a cat," Bernie chimed in. "That's for sure."

"Come on, kitty," Jason said, standing under the branch and calling up to the cat, trying to entice her down with a snap of his fingers and a piece of cheese. "Come on and join the party."

Lily looked at him intently, stood on the branch and wriggled, arching her back and stretching out her front paws as she did when she was happy.

Jason clapped his hands, getting her attention. "Good cat. Come down."

Lily looked away, flicked her tail a few times, then returned her attention to Jason. Like a flash, she leapt from the branch and landed on his head, knocking him on his derriere. With a panicky squawk, she scrambled her paws like she was treading water to get away from him, kicking the wig from his head.

Jason sat on the grass with a dazed look, his wig on the ground next to him while the cat ran into the kitchen through the door Lindsey had left open.

"Good girl!" Lindsey said as Lily barreled across the kitchen floor and into the living room. Finally, the wig was off. She suddenly realized what had really happened. "I mean, bad girl!" She ran out the back door.

Jason, wig in hand, stood up and was smoothing the wild locks of blond hair with his fingers.

"Are you okay?" Lindsey placed a hand on his shoulder. "I'm so sorry! Lily has absolutely no manners!" *And she made me the happiest woman in town*, Lindsey refrained from adding.

"I'm fine," Jason said. "Luckily, all the dancing has given me a firm behind to cushion the blow."

"She didn't scratch you, did she?" Lindsey took Jason's chin in her hand and moved his head from side to side, inspecting him for claw marks. "No scratches or nicks." She couldn't keep her eyes off his head and fought to restrain her smile when his hair blew slightly in the easy breeze and flickered in the sun.

He raised up the limp, black wig. "Cat claws are no match for this!"

"Sorry." Lindsey lifted her eyes apologetically. "Hope you're not upset she knocked off your . . ."

"You're the best doctor in town, but I don't know if there's anything you can do to revive this!" Jason waved his wig in the air and put his head back, laughing heartily.

She couldn't tear her eyes away from his real hair.

"Something wrong up there?" He placed his hand on the top of his head.

"Sorry," she said, lowering her eyes from his hair. "It's just that I . . . I never saw your . . . your real hair."

Jason's face broke out into a good-natured grin. "Guess you haven't. So, what's your professional opinion, Doctor?"

Lindsey couldn't help smiling at his easy manner. Most people would have been mortified to be knocked to the ground and scalped by a cat. "Love it!" She clasped her hands and wished she'd contained her enthusiasm a little. "Blond becomes you." She reached up and smoothed down a few wayward strands.

"Coming from a redhead, I'll take that as a compliment!" he joked.

"So, do you feel . . . naked . . . without your wig?" It was really none of her business, but she'd been waiting a long time for this moment.

He wrinkled his forehead. "Lindsey, you do know I only wear the wigs and the costumes when I perform, right? I mean, I didn't take off the wig before I came here because if someone other than you and Tom were to come to the door and see me in the costume and no wig, well, that might destroy the illusion for a fan. I figure it's always best to be the whole fantasy or no fantasy at all."

She nodded and suppressed her desire to give him a big hug for finally saying the words she'd been wanting to hear.

"Maybe you like me better with the wig," he said with a devilish twinkle in his eye. "Without this," he said, shaking the wig, "Elvis ceases to be. And for anyone who falls for Elvis, Jason can be a real letdown."

Did Jason think she'd fallen for him? Or Elvis? No, he was probably just talking in generalities. "Elvis could ever compete with the real Jason," she said with a smile.

Lindsey sensed a momentary awkwardness, the uneasiness of meeting someone for the first time and trying to keep that thunderbolt attraction to a dull roar so you wouldn't appear so transparent. Suddenly, her patient was gone, Elvis was gone, the man behind the flowers was gone. She stood in her own backyard with an unexpected stranger whom she had been longing to meet. And who had been worth the wait. Now what?

Jason looked at her and winked. "Let's get that food on the grill." He took her by the hand and led her into the house.

"Darndest thing I ever saw." Lindsey heard Tom say to Bernie through the screen door. "The boy's hair came right off his head! Things are finally getting interesting around here!"

Chapter Nine

"Two pieces are my limit, Doc." Bernie held up his hand in refusal when Lindsey offered him another piece of pie. "Dee-licious."

"You can thank the bakery department at the A&P for that!" she said. "Anyone else?"

Tom and Jason shook their heads and pushed away their plates.

"A few more meals like that, and I'll end up imitating the old, fat Elvis." Jason tugged at this belt. "The young Elvis seems to be everyone's favorite."

"Well, Doc," Bernie said, pulling a toothpick from his breast pocket and placing it in his mouth. "Again you've been more than kind by fixin' this wonderful meal for us. The only way to properly thank you is to let Jason perform for your care center benefit. Have you given any more thought to our offer?"

Lindsey's shoulders dropped, and she pushed her fingers through her hair, hesitating before speaking. "I really appreciate your most generous offer," she said, shifting her eyes from Bernie to Jason, "but we couldn't ask you to perform for free. I mean, that's your livelihood. It would be asking way too much."

Bernie raised his hand. "Now that's just nonsense, Doc. Jason and I talked about this, and it would mean a lot to us now, and maybe some day in the future, if you would let us put on a show."

Lindsey turned to Jason and raised her eyebrows. She wasn't sure what some day in the future meant. "Far be it from me to say no to The King," she said, unable to force her tone to be more convincing.

"Well, okay, then," Bernie said, standing and patting his stomach. "Glad that's settled. I need to move a little or I'm going to burst right out of these pants," he smirked. "Tom, how about you get in that chair of yours and let me take you for a spin around the block? We'll leave the young ones to clean up while us old guys get out of their way."

"As long as you have me back by midnight," Tom laughed. "That's when my wheelchair turns into a pumpkin."

"Well, if that happens, we'll make a great big pie and eat ourselves into another frenzy," Bernie joked as he helped Tom into the house to get the wheelchair.

The screen door fluttered closed with a few short slaps, sounding louder in the quiet that engulfed Lindsey and Jason. The trees cast waning shadows on the ground, and the birds' songs were becoming intermittent as they started to quiet for the night. A few tree frogs chirped, and that unmistakable, peaceful feeling of a summer evening started to descend. The purest and most innocent bliss.

Jason rose from his seat across from Lindsey at the picnic table, walked around the green wooden benches, and sat next to her, close enough to cause her to stiffen. It was difficult to discern the heat of his body from the heat of the evening.

"Thanks for letting me do the show for your care center," he said.

"I'm the one who should be thanking you," she replied, curious about why he seemed so eager to do this performance. "You're sharing your time and talent for nothing." She turned to him and wondered why she hadn't noticed the few freckles dusting the top of his cheekbones.

"Not for nothing. It's important to me." He shuffled his foot in the grass.

"Why?"

"A couple of reasons." Jason held up a finger. "First, it will help you with a cause that means a lot to you and the people of Owl Cove. This town feels like home to me now, so I'm happy to help out." He held up a second finger. "And, who knows, some day down the road, my brother may need a place to stay."

"Your brother?" She flashed back to the little boy in the picture she'd seen at Jason's apartment.

"Kevin has been living in St. John's Nursing Home for the past year," Jason began. "Some of the nurses told me the home may close in a year or so. Then I'll have to find another place for him. If the care center doesn't open, we'll probably have to move."

Move? The word shot a trickle of anxiety through her. "That explains all of Elvis's appearances at St. John's."

He nodded. "Yeah, Kev really gets a kick out of seeing me in costume. I don't even know if he remembers what the real me looks like."

Lindsey put her hand on Jason's arm. "Tell me about him," she said, blending her medical curiosity with a need to know more about Jason's life. "You never mentioned him before."

Jason lowered his head. "It's just family stuff I can't imagine interests most people."

"I'm not most people," Lindsey said firmly. "I'm your doctor and your friend. Someone who cares about you."

Jason took her hands in his. "Kevin is my younger brother. Four years younger. He's mentally and physically challenged. Born that way."

"Sorry to hear that." Lindsey felt Jason grasp her hands tighter.

"My mother couldn't accept his disabilities. Made

her go over the edge. When Kevin was a year old, she left us. Last I knew she moved to France where she married some guy."

"Wow." Lindsey saw the hurt in his eyes. "That had to be tough to deal with."

"When you're a kid, things just are as they are. That blind innocence is really a gift. Hey, what do you say we get these cleared away?" He motioned to the dirty dishes on the table.

"I'll do it later," Lindsey said.

Jason was already on his feet and gathering the glasses. "Let me help. When I was a kid, some of my happiest times were spent standing at the sink with my dad while he washed and I dried."

"Okay, then. You'll have to let me know how I stack up as a dishwasher."

They piled the dishes on a tray and carried them into the kitchen. Lindsey filled half of the split sink with detergent and water, placed in the dirty dishes, then set the rinsed dishes in the other half for Jason to dry. He stood close to her, handling each dish carefully and drying it more thoroughly than Lindsey ever had. One of her least favorite household tasks had suddenly become interesting, at least as an observer, and she regretted that she had only a few dishes to wash. She felt her face flush, and she wasn't sure if the steam from the water or having Jason so close to her was to blame.

"Why is Kevin in St. John's?" Lindsey asked.

"We grew up in Albany, at the other end of the state,"

he began. "When our father became sick about five years ago, Kevin was put into a facility there. I was working and trying to care for Dad, and Kev needed more than we could do for him at home."

"That's a tough choice to make," Lindsey said, wondering if she'd ever have to make that same decision about her grandfather.

"Then our father died, so Kevin became my responsibility. When his condition worsened about a year ago, his doctor suggested that he be transferred to St. John's because of their expertise with his disability."

Lindsey nodded enthusiastically. "Dr. Raymore?"

"You know her?" Jason's face lit up.

"For sure. I worked with her one summer when I was in med school. Good move to put Kevin in her program. She's the best."

"He's getting good care." Jason held up a glass to the light to check for water spots. "I'm really impressed with St. John's and all that Dr. Raymore has done for him."

"That's why you moved here?" A bubble of detergent floated upward onto Lindsey's nose, and Jason reached over and wiped it off. Such pleasure from a simple touch.

"Kevin needs to be close to Elvis."

Lindsey looked directly at Jason. "Elvis?"

"Elvis," Jason repeated.

Lindsey pulled the plug in the sink, and the water and suds spiraled down the drain with a sucking sound.

She dried her hands on the towel Jason handed her. "Thanks for your help. Let's sit on the porch and get some air."

When she opened the front door, Jingle and Lily scurried out. Jingle curled up on her rug, and Lily straddled the railing, waiting for Lindsey to take her usual seat on the swing. Lindsey lit the candle on the porch table, and she and Jason settled into the swing. She couldn't remember the last time she'd shared that seat with anyone.

Lily jumped into Lindsey's lap, sniffed at Jason, and then walked over to him and curled up.

"I think she's trying to say she's sorry," Lindsey chuckled at the wide-eyed look on Jason's face as he covered his head with his hands in exaggerated terror.

He rubbed the cat under her chin. "As long as she doesn't try to use my head as a scratching post. Without the wig, that would not tickle."

They sat in silence for a few moments. Jason anchored his foot on the porch floor and slowly pushed the swing back and forth. With each push, he seemed to inch closer to Lindsey. Their arms touched so even Lily's flapping tail didn't fit between them.

"Pretty, isn't it?" commented Jason, looking at the sky that was turning a muted shade of gray and pink as the sun dipped further. Thin streams of gray clouds zigzagged across the sky.

"A sight to behold," said Lindsey lazily.

"Certainly is." Jason turned to her. "It's almost the prettiest thing in my line of vision."

Despite the warm evening, Lindsey felt a chill that started like a tiny tickle and grew into a convulsion, like the ripple left by a pebble tossed into a pond. She inhaled deeply and savored the scent of the gardenias in the flowerboxes and the subtle cologne Jason was wearing. She wanted to close her eyes and let time stop for just this moment as she centered herself and enjoyed the aura of the fascinating man sitting next to her.

"Fireflies," Jason said, pointing to little blips of light flashing by the front pine tree. "Cool."

"Those remind me of being a kid. Grandpa and I used to sit right here and see who could count the most. The winner got an extra cookie. Funny, I always seemed to count one more than he did." She smiled at the memory.

"When my father took Kevin and me in his truck, we'd stop at a rest stop to sleep. Sometimes in the middle of the night, I'd wake up to see Kevin staring out the window, a big clownish smile on his face as he watched the fireflies in the trees on the roadside."

"Your father had a truck?" Lindsey recalled the photo, another piece of the puzzle.

The cat walked over to Lindsey's lap for a few strokes before jumping back onto the railing.

"Yeah, he was a long-distance trucker between Albany and Memphis. On school vacations, he often took us with him. It was great. Driving for hours, pulling the horn, eating at truck stops, sleeping in the cab." Jason nodded. "Good times."

"Did Kevin like it?" Lindsey slipped off her shoes, turned sideways to face Jason, and tucked her feet under her dress.

"Sure did. He didn't engage too deeply with most things, but we could always tell when he was having fun. He still gets this silly little grin and claps his hands when he's happy."

"Cute," said Lindsey, touched at Jason's devotion to his brother and thinking of the face she'd seen in the picture.

"Not too many things would evoke a reaction from Kevin, but when we used to drive to Memphis, he would really respond to images and sounds of Elvis. It was really strange. I have no idea why Elvis made him so happy."

Lindsey nodded. "I think I do."

Jason swallowed hard. "Ever since Kev was a baby, Dad and I tried anything and everything to get him to show us that something was going on inside that head of his. No luck. Then one day on the way to Memphis he saw a billboard with Elvis's picture on it and his face lit up like a firecracker. We thought it was just a reflex until he heard an Elvis song on the radio. He tried to sing along, mumbling the words and even moving slightly. Really weird. Some of the top specialists in the country couldn't get a reaction from him like Elvis could."

Lindsey felt a fluttering sensation in her stomach that traveled throughout her body as the picture came into focus. "So that's why you pretend to be Elvis. For your brother."

He nodded. "After a trip to Memphis, days, weeks would go by when Kevin would just sit in his wheelchair, staring into space. Then one day I remembered how he acted when he saw Elvis. So I put on my aunt's black wig and my father's old suit and lip synced to an Elvis record. It was like I raised my brother from the dead."

She reached over and touched his hair, the soft blond strands feeling silky between her fingers. She was sorry for wrongly judging the impersonator who had stumbled into her ER. She wanted to take back the frustration she felt with his silly costumes and her loathsome attitude toward his wig. Jason had to be the most unselfish man she'd ever met. "Now I get it," she said, tugging his hair.

He reached for her hand. "I know the whole thing is a little kooky. When Kevin went to the facility in Albany, I used to stop there and perform for him all the time, just to keep him stimulated. It got so that people used to wait for me to visit so they could see the show. One day, Bernie was there spending time with his neighbor and he saw my act. He used to run a radio station in Nashville, and he had some good connections. I guess he was impressed because he told me if I decided take my show on the road, he'd be my manager."

"He's done a good job," Lindsey replied. "You're the

headliner around this town, that's for sure!" *And in my heart*, she wanted to add.

"I promised Kevin some day I'd perform in Las Vegas, just for him. When I said that, in his own garbled speech, I'm sure he said, 'Brother is my star.' "

"No pressure there," Lindsey said, straightening her dress.

"Tell me about it." Jason rolled his eyes. "We all need a goal. And I have to admit, life on the stage is more exciting than being an accountant. I guess Kevin helped me find my calling."

Lindsey felt his grip tighten.

"And all of that led me to Owl Cove, where I wrenched my back and found myself at the mercy of an emergency room doctor with the greenest eyes and bounciest curls I've ever seen."

Lindsey cleared her throat and batted her eyelashes. "I hope she took good care of you."

"Treatment fit for a king!" Jason replied.

Chapter Ten

When Lindsey pulled in her driveway at eight o'clock the next evening, she was surprised to see Jason sitting on her front step. What didn't surprise her, unfortunately, was the Elvis gear.

"Hi, there," he said, walking over to the car to meet her.

Her keys slipped from her hands when she stepped out of the car. "Good to see you."

Jason bent to scoop up the keys. "Butter fingers today?" He dangled the keys in front of her.

She shuddered. "Wish that was the only problem." She touched the collar of her white coat and huffed. "Don't tell me I still have this on. Where is my head at?" She bounced the ball of her hand on her temple.

"Tough day at the shop?"

"Tough doesn't even begin to describe it." She

113

reached for a fistful of her hair and pulled, opening her mouth and pretending to scream.

"What's up?"

They walked up the steps to the front door, and Lindsey held her keyring up to the porch light to identify the housekey.

"I stopped by about an hour ago after I left my show for the Little League Parents' Guild. I just wanted to thank you for dinner last night. And for listening to me. I had a really, really special time."

She touched his arm. "Grandpa and I really enjoyed your and Bernie's company. All he talked about before he went to bed was that stroll Bernie took him on and Bernie's stories of the old days at his radio station and all the celebrities he'd met. Grandpa was starstruck!"

Lindsey unlocked the front door, and they were greeted by the thundering feet of Jingle and Lily. "Come in. You've been sitting on the step for an hour?" Jason's words were just sinking in. She turned on a few lamps to brighten the dark house.

"I didn't mind. It's such a nice evening. I wasn't surprised you weren't home, but I thought for sure Tom would be here."

Lindsey turned to Jason, opened her mouth to speak, and started to cry. Slow, watery trickles down her cheeks.

"What's wrong?" he asked.

She hung her head to hide her face. The tears flowed harder, and she tried to wipe them away with the back of her hand.

Jason reached out and touched her arm. "Lindsey, tell me what's wrong?"

"Grandpa's in the hospital," she said amongst sobs.

He led her to the couch, took a tissue from the box on the table, and handed it to her.

Her body heaved from the sobs, great releases of tension and fear. "He couldn't breathe well this morning when he woke up. Bad asthma attack. So I admitted him."

Jason pulled another tissue from the box. Instead of handing it to her, he wiped her tears himself. "Is he okay?"

She straightened up and tried to compose herself. Crying wasn't something she was accustomed to doing. She just didn't. Couldn't. She was the physician, the one with a good head on her shoulders. The rock. Not this time. It never failed. On those rare occasions when she let her emotions run free, they took off on her, a force of their own just waiting to escape.

Through watery eyes, she saw the surreal image of Elvis offering her comfort. Jason's features weren't crystal clear, but Elvis's wig couldn't be mistaken. "He'll be fine," she said with a quiver as she regained her composure. "This has happened before. If he weren't a month shy of turning ninety, I wouldn't have admitted him at all. Maybe I overreacted."

"It's best to be careful." Jason kept a tight grip on her hand.

She dabbed at her eyes. "Sorry for . . . for this."

Lindsey gestured to herself. "It's just been one of those days where everything went wrong. First Grandpa scared the heck out of me. Then the ER was going crazy. Then a bird almost ran into my car when I was driving home. Then—"

"Shh," Jason said, putting an arm around her shoulder. "Everything will be all right."

"I usually don't—"

"I know," he interrupted. "You're the one everyone leans on."

She sniffed again and nodded.

"But you're not a one-woman show, Lindsey. You have to learn to let others help you. Let me."

If she could only count the times she'd heard that throughout the years. After her parents died in an accident when she was four and she moved in with her widowed grandfather, the self-sufficiency kicked in big time. When her age was still a single digit, she was doing the housework, taking in every stray animal that walked up their path, and running errands for the elderly neighbors. She remembered her grandfather telling her she was a little bundle of energy, but one day her steam would run out if she didn't watch it.

The more Lindsey did, the more she needed to do. When she told her grandfather she wanted to become a doctor, he said he wasn't surprised. Taking care of people was what she did best. Lindsey would never let anyone down—only herself.

"Hah," Lindsey said. "I have a nerve to complain to you of all people about too many obligations. You're such a hero to your brother."

"Not a hero, Lindsey. Just someone who's doing what he has to do."

She sniffled again. Had he any idea that he was her hero too?

"You going to be okay here alone tonight? I . . . I believe I do owe a favor to the person who stayed up with me all night when I clunked my head."

"I'll be fine," she said, unable to convince herself. The last thing she needed was for Elvis to take care of her. If she let him, she'd have to face the music, literally. "I'm just going to turn in early and sleep off this day."

Jason stood to leave. "I'll leave you alone so you can crash. Call if you need anything."

As he headed out the door and down the front steps, blending into the darkness, he turned to her. "Don't be so hard on yourself. Things aren't always as they seem."

Yes, despite all the confusion swimming through her head, the one thing that she was totally sure of since meeting Jason Kincaid was that things certainly weren't always as they seemed.

"He offered to stay with you? All night?" Mary questioned Lindsey's words. She flashed her friend an exaggerated wink and placed her hand to her mouth in a fake expression of shock.

"No, no. It wasn't like that," Lindsey said as she and Mary made their way through the cashier's line in the hospital cafeteria. "Jason is a perfect gentleman."

Lindsey carried the tray containing her tea and Mary's coffee and banana muffin to a table in the corner.

"But is Elvis?" asked Mary. "That's the real question. Not from what I read in the tabloids!"

Lindsey couldn't help chuckling. "Don't tell me you're confusing them now too!"

"Kind of hard not to!" Mary took a bite of her muffin.

"I used to think that," Lindsey said. "But I was wrong. Jason is so sweet and genuine, so unpretentious. And so devoted to his brother." She took a sip from the steaming cup. "He's not at all like his alter ego, not at all. In fact, if you take away the wig, he doesn't even look like him."

"Then what's stopping you?" Mary stirred three sugar packets into her coffee.

"Stopping me?"

"Yeah, from getting out of that safe haven you've created for yourself and giving the guy a chance. From all accounts, he's certainly interested. I'd bet the farm he'd ask you out if he thought you'd accept."

Lindsey rested her head in her hand. "Sometimes I get that feeling, but I don't know."

Mary shook her head. "You better prescribe yourself some anti-stick-in-the-mud pills. The guy is so into you."

"Probably not."

"And you're into him."

"Who can ever really be sure?"

Mary threw down her coffee stirrer on the tray. "I give up. How can a woman who was valedictorian of her high school class and in the top five of her med school be so dumb?"

Lindsey sat up and shot Mary a glance. "I am not dumb!"

"Then you're afraid," Mary countered quickly.

"No, I'm not," Lindsey said, the exchange reminding her of their teenage bantering.

Lindsey's shoulders slumped, and she put her head back, exasperated with her friend's doggedness. "Okay, okay," she relented. "I admit it. I like Jason, a lot. And I can tell he likes me. But I'm a doctor, for goodness' sake. I can't date Elvis Presley!" Her voice elevated a little, prompting an interested look from a few people at the next table.

Lindsey's pager buzzed, and she looked at the device hanging on her pocket. "Grandpa!"

Lindsey and Mary tore out of the cafeteria and ran to Tom's room. They found him attached to an oxygen mask, eyes closed, unresponsive, and surrounded by nurses who were frantically attending to him and waiting for Lindsey to arrive.

Leaving Tom's room, Lindsey took a deep breath. She leaned against the wall and rotated her head, releasing the tension in her shoulders. "Close one," she said to Mary. "I don't even want to think about what could have happened if he were alone at home when he had an asthma attack like that one."

Mary patted her friend's shoulder. "Take it easy. He's stable. The old guy has a lot of fight." She smirked. "Kind of like his granddaughter."

Lindsey's head was spinning. "He's going to need more care. Maybe not today or tomorrow, but eventually. He's quickly reaching the point where he can't be left alone."

"What are you thinking?" asked Mary, her voice gentle, probing.

"He needs the care center."

Mary nodded.

"And I have to make sure that the center comes to be."

"Well, the benefit is next week. That's a big step. All you need for that to happen is Jason."

"Actually," said Lindsey her mouth turning into an impish grin, "I really need Elvis."

Chapter Eleven

"Looks like we're all set for the show tomorrow," Lindsey said to the committee as they closed their meeting.

"Pre-sale tickets are very strong, very strong indeed," said Sanjay, as he consulted his notebook. "We've already sold one thousand eight hundred and forty. And the capacity of the high school auditorium is only two thousand."

"Should be a sellout," Enrique added. "Standing room only!"

"All I know is I'll be in the front row," said Julie, dancing in her seat. "I won't miss a trick, and I plan to sing along with every song."

"This could be the event of the season in Owl Cove!"

Mary chirped, clapping her hands. "I can't wait. I wonder how many costume changes Jason will have?"

"I can't wait to give Henry the final tally from the ticket sales," said Lindsey. "That should put us pretty close to where we need to be to break ground on the care center." She held up both hands with crossed fingers.

"So much good has happened so quickly, no?" Enrique commented.

"You might say that," Lindsey replied, thinking of the many conversations she had with Jason about the show over the last couple of weeks.

Jason made up excuses to stop by her house to talk about the show, always accompanied by a box of cookies, a gallon of ice cream, or some other treat. A few times he showed up at the hospital to meet her for lunch, in full costume, after a visit to his brother. And a day didn't go by when he missed phoning her for no other reason than to say how much he was looking forward to doing the show. His enthusiasm was endless. When Lindsey found herself buying an Elvis CD at the music store last week, she knew the tide was turning—rapidly.

After the meeting, Lindsey walked down the hall with Julie, who was wearing an I Love Elvis button on her Looney Tunes scrubs.

"So how did you get to be such a big Elvis fan?" Lindsey asked.

"Oh, it's a family thing," Julie said. "My mother loved Elvis, and she passed it down to my sisters and me. When I was a kid, Elvis music was always playing in the house. We used to dance in the living room to 'Viva Las Vegas,' 'Suspicious Minds,' 'Are You Lonesome Tonight?,' all his hits." She smiled. "My mother even wore the black Priscilla beehive for a while!"

"Sounds like Elvis played a big role in your life," Lindsey added.

"I'll say. We even had a couple family vacations to Graceland. In our house, there was no doubt Elvis was The King." She hummed "Blue Hawaii." "Elvis, fun, and happiness—they were all rolled into one."

"So that's why you like listening to Jason so much? The memories?" Lindsey was asking questions like a well-trained reporter, trying hard to fully understand the Elvis magic, build her connection to Jason.

"That and because he's a good entertainer." Julie paused at the desk to pick up her charts. "Seeing him helps take away some of the sting I remember when the real Elvis died. Was that ever a dark day in our house! My mother had us all crying like babies." She shuddered at the memory. "Jason keeps the fun alive."

"Really?" Lindsey was surprised to hear anyone attached to a celebrity. Lindsey certainly had her share of celebrity crushes when she was growing up, but it was never an obsession as it seemed to be with so many dedicated Elvis followers.

Julie nodded. "Life without Elvis was very sad. He

had something special that was hard to put your finger on, if you know what I mean."

Lindsey nodded. "I know exactly what you mean."

The committee and their guests occupied front row seats that gave Lindsey the opportunity to observe Jason at his finest. She watched with captivated interest and a newfound curiosity while he wriggled, shook, spun, and twisted through all of his numbers, smiling and working the crowd like a seasoned performer. He danced and sang tirelessly through three sets, bringing to life a variety of songs, each one more captivating than the last.

She was mesmerized at the performer . . . and the man. She wondered if the rest of the audience thought he looked her way a little too often and if he hovered near her side of the stage, their gazes locked, during the tender songs. Yes, something extraordinary happened on that stage. But something more magical happened in Lindsey's heart and soul.

When Jason sang and sauntered through the audience, draping scarves on the women, Lindsey watched with fascination as the female fans swooned and cooed, longing for a chance to touch him, connect. Whether for a lifetime or for just the few minutes that the song lasted, Jason made a tremendous impact on their lives. And if she hadn't had the opportunity to come to know him over the last few weeks, she would have been baffled by the whole scene.

When Jason approached Lindsey's seat and presented her with a scarf and a peck on the cheek, she felt giddy with excitement and was as surprised at the change in herself as she was at his transformation into this icon. Watching him perform transported her into another world, a world where she was free to show her fascination with the man. Where she wasn't Lindsey, the physician who had an image to maintain. Where she was just a woman charmed by an enigmatic man who had unlocked a portion of her soul.

By the time the show was over, Lindsey was floating. She could barely pull herself together enough to meet with the committee and count the proceeds from the ticket sales. When Sanjay tallied the count from the last dollar, the committee cheered at the hefty amount. That was surely enough to convince the board of directors that the care center project was alive and well. Lindsey hurried to find Jason and thank him again for his generosity, but he had already left. She wasn't sure if she could bear to wait until tomorrow to talk to him.

By the time she and Tom returned home, both were happily exhausted from laughing and singing, not only at the show but on the ride home too. "That Jason is certainly sweet on you," Tom said as they entered the house after the show.

Lindsey was taken aback by his statement and pleased her grandfather had actually made the distinction between Jason and Elvis this time. "I don't think so," she replied, her face still frozen with the smile that had been plastered on it all night.

"Regardless of what you think, that's a fact," Tom said, as they headed into his bedroom.

"Oh, Grandpa." Lindsey pulled his pajamas out of the drawer and lay them on the bed.

"He'd be a darn fool not to notice a girl like you."

" 'Night, Grandpa," Lindsey said, wondering if maybe, just maybe, there was some truth to his words.

"And you'd be a darn fool not to let him!"

She kissed her grandfather and closed the door behind her. She put the stereo on low and popped in her new Elvis CD. Alone in the candlelit darkness of her living room, with sounds of the real Elvis humming softly in the background, she enjoyed the aftershocks of a terrific evening as she thought of her king.

She danced around the room, her head full of tunes and images from the show and her heart bursting from the excitement of seeing Jason perform. With all the adrenaline surging through her, there was no way she could go to sleep.

Just before ten-thirty, as Lindsey was reaching to turn off the lamp and go to bed, she heard a knock at the front door. She furrowed her brow and hurried to the door, peering out the small eye-level window. Jason! Dressed as Jason! His blond hair shone under the porch light.

She unlocked the door and opened it.

"I know it's late," he said quickly.

"Everything okay?" His history of catastrophes

flashed through her mind. She stepped aside as he entered.

"Sorry I wasn't able to see you after the show. I had to do a little interview for the local news."

"Wow! You really are a celebrity!" Lindsey said, her tone light and playful. "Hope you won't forget me when you're famous."

"That'll be the day!" Jason retorted. "For fame or forgetting." He winked. "Hope the show turned out okay."

"Okay? It was phenomenal! I've never had such fun in my life!" She gave him a quick hug. "Thank you."

"Did you meet your goal for the care center?"

"I think so. Henry will give a report to the board tomorrow, so we should know soon. But I think your show put us over the top." She stretched out her arms and hugged him again, not in such a hurry to break free this time.

Lindsey's eyes met his. She felt breathless, and if she'd had her stethoscope, she would have been able to prove her heart was beating at warp speed. What was this man doing to her?

"I thought the best part of the show was seeing you from the stage. Seeing that fun look on your face and watching you smile," Jason said, taking both her hands. "But I was wrong."

"Wrong?"

"The best part is now, when the show is over. Sharing this moment with the most beautiful member of the audience. Being here with you, Lindsey. With only you."

They moved to the couch and sat closely, holding each others' hands, no words spoken. In the silence, she had never felt so complete. The serenity of the evening, the dim light in the room, the soft sounds of Elvis on the stereo, the electricity that transcended the universe—all working just for the two of them.

"You'll be quite the hero at the hospital when the care center is built," Jason finally said, breaking the silence. "I'm happy for you."

"I'm happy for everyone who will benefit from the care center. You've helped more people than you'll ever know." She squeezed his hand.

"Think there'll be a place for Kevin there, if he ever needs it?" A look of concern clouded his face.

"Of course. And for Grandpa and anyone else who needs a home."

Jason nodded slowly. "Home sounds good. That's something I miss."

She snapped her head toward him. His poignant tone concerned her. "But you have a home."

"No, I have a place where I live. Big difference." He looked around the room and extended his arms. "This is a home."

Lindsey has been so caught up in worrying about how to stop caring for this person with the crazy profession that she had totally overlooked the man. His only family was a special needs brother, and he lived in a tiny three-room apartment. Of course he longed for a home. What would she do if she couldn't come home after an exhausting day of work to her grandfather, pets, and porch swing? Those were her anchors.

"Ever think you'll have a family and a home of your own?" Jason asked. "I mean, other than Tom."

"Maybe someday." She wasn't about to bare her soul and admit that lately the prospect of that happening seemed more remote than ever. "You?"

"Maybe someday."

They sat again in silence, Lindsey relaxing as she leaned a little closer to him. He felt so warm, so comfortable. She rested her head on his shoulder and the softness of his cotton shirt, fresh with the scent of lavender detergent, embraced her. The perfect moment in a perfect night.

"Problem is," Jason continued, tilting his head so that it rested on hers, "I tend to be a little, uh, accident prone."

"No!" she exclaimed, exaggerating her surprise.

"Believe it or not, yes," he joked. "And that special woman I find will have to be able to tend to all my bumps and bruises. Know anyone like that?"

"I've heard of such people," she said, holding back a snicker.

"Plus there's this Elvis impersonating thing I do. I imagine lots of women find that to be a little, well, off the wall."

"From what I saw tonight, looks like a lot of women would like the chance to romance The King." Lindsey held back a giggle. "The wig is very alluring."

Jason tweaked her nose.

"My guy will have to put up with my demanding profession and spoiled pets. Not an easy thing to ask a man to do."

"Well, your cat may be a hard sell, but the right man will be proud of your accomplishments and support your career."

Jason raised his hand and touched Lindsey's head. "These curls are just fantastic." He turned his face to hers, lifting her chin with his finger, inching closer to her lips.

"Lindsey, you still up?" Tom called from the bedroom.

She bolted upright, startled to hear her grandfather's call and in a fog from the fantasy of whatever could have transpired.

"Lindsey, you out there?" Tom called again.

"What do you need, Grandpa?" He didn't sound like he was gasping for breath, like another asthma attack was in progress.

"An aspirin. My tooth is bothering me again."

"Be right there." Lindsey gave Jason an apologetic grin. "The tooth his bridge connects to has been sensitive. He has a dentist appointment tomorrow." She bopped her hand on her head. "That reminds me—I need to call Mary and tell her I'll be late for work."

"Time for me to go anyway." Jason stood and pulled Lindsey to her feet. "Thanks for your company."

They walked toward the door, hand in hand.

"Say, want me to take your grandfather to the dentist tomorrow?"

Lindsey smiled and shook her head. "No, but thanks for offering." He had already done too much. If he started to tend to her family, well, that would just make everything harder to sort out. Already, she didn't know what to make of things.

"I'm available, and you wouldn't have to miss work." He opened his eyes widely, waiting for her reply.

She was wavering. She could sure use a hand with Tom, but the possibility of Jason showing up dressed as Elvis loomed. That would throw her grandfather for a loop.

And disappoint her.

"The appointment is at nine. You don't have a show right before or after, do you?" She bit her lip waiting for his reply and a hint about what he'd be wearing.

"No show at all tomorrow. As I said, I'm free."

"Well, okay then. I'll tell Grandpa you'll be here around eight forty-five."

Jason moved closer to her, as if in slow motion, his gaze locked on her, his target clear. She waited, anticipating a kiss from his tender lips, the feeling of that joy already starting to surge through her. She closed her eyes and breathed in his linen-fresh scent, opening her lips an almost imperceptible distance.

Then Tom called out again, and her eyes flew open and she jerked back her head. "Lindsey, can you bring my heating pad too?"

They looked at each other and smiled. Yes, they would

have other opportunities, but this moment had passed. One split second in the span of time that may have altered their world forever.

"Be right there," she called to Tom and loosened her grip on Jason's hands.

She and Jason didn't exchange another word, and he blew her a kiss from his fingertips as he walked out the door. Not the same, but a gesture that made her tingle nonetheless.

As she closed the door, Tom called out again. "Did he kiss you?"

Lindsey guessed that her grandfather's mouth would be sore from the dentist, so she left him a bowl of soup needing only to be microwaved. He should have been able to handle that, but she hurried home during her lunch hour to check on him anyway.

She walked through the front door and stopped short. Jason and her grandfather were eating submarine sandwiches on TV trays in the living room.

"Here comes the doctor," Jason said, standing to greet her. The real Jason, not Elvis.

"So am I invited to the party?" she joked, noting the smile on her grandfather's face.

"I'd say you are the party." Jason wiped his mouth with his napkin.

"Hardly," she said, rolling her eyes. "No one shows up to a party the way I'm dressed." She pointed to the spots on her white coat. "I dropped a bottle of orange cough medicine on this sleeve. And then a patient flinched when I was cleaning her wound with antiseptic and knocked it on my collar." She put her finger through a hole by her pocket. "A scared little boy grabbed my nametag and made a run for it."

"What's the brown stain?" asked Tom, pointing to the front of the coat.

Lindsey grimaced and raised her eyes shyly. "Coffee. Uh, I did that."

"Well, you know what they say: it's not a party until something gets spilled," Jason added with a laugh.

"So how was the dentist?" She looked at the sandwich her grandfather was chomping on. Apparently, he was able to handle more than soup.

"Choppers are as good as new," Tom replied, showing his teeth. "Jason even gave a little show for some scared lady in the waiting room. What a hoot!"

Lindsey turned to Jason. "You put on a show at the dentist? Without your costume?"

He waved away her comment. "Some poor woman was so nervous to be getting her tooth pulled that she was almost in tears. So I sang a little song to cheer her up. No big deal."

"He had the whole place hoppin'!" Tom took another big bite of his sandwich and dripped mayonnaise on his shirt.

"It was a big deal to the woman whose nerves you soothed," Lindsey smiled. Jason didn't have a medical degree, but he was apparently a natural healer.

"Oh, your sub is in the refrigerator," Jason said. "Thought you'd be hungry. Tom said you like tuna."

"Why, she never slows down long enough to have a decent meal." Tom stuffed a few potato chips in his mouth. "She'll get skinny as a rail at this rate."

"That will be the day! I wish I could drop five pounds," said Lindsey.

Jason shook his head. "You can't improve on perfection."

Lindsey smiled shyly. *Perfect* was one word she never used to describe herself. Growing up, she was the proverbial ugly duckling. When all the other girls in her class tossed about their long, silky manes, Lindsey was fighting a crop of red curls that made her look like a cross between Orphan Annie and Bozo the Clown on a humid day. During grade school, she was taller than most of the boys. Add braces on her teeth and a pair of glasses to the mix, and she thought herself to be the least attractive thing on knobby knees.

In high school, she had seen a picture of her mother taken a year before she died. A young woman in her twenties, she had a bright smile, beautiful soft red curls, and sparkling eyes. "Know what made your mother so beautiful?" Tom had asked when he walked in on her staring at the photo.

"Everything," Lindsey had answered, lisping through her braces and wondering why she hadn't taken a dip in that gene pool.

"Her attitude," Tom had replied. "Sure, she had pretty

features, but she loved life so much it was like the sun was shining inside her all the time."

"Think I'll ever be that pretty?" Lindsey had asked.

"You already are," Tom had said. "Now as soon as you start believing that, everyone else will see it too."

Lindsey remembered that day as a turning point in her life. The day when she realized she was in control of her destiny. The day the sun started to shine for her.

She blushed at Jason's comment. "Thanks for the sandwich. I'll take it back to work." She needed to get out of the house quickly. Jason seemed too comfortable, like he'd always been here. Like he was part of her life. Like he had almost kissed her and had come to finish the job. Like she wanted him to.

It had been easy to turn her back on Elvis, but the man standing before her, the man who fit so perfectly into this day, this home—her life—was almost impossible to resist. If she gave in, life would be fine . . . until Elvis reappeared. And then what? Lindsey couldn't endure the thought of Jason choosing between Elvis and her. She wasn't so sure who he might pick.

"Want a ride?" Jason asked.

"No, thanks. You've already done too much."

Chapter Twelve

Henry jumped to his feet and walked around the desk to shake Lindsey's hand. He pumped her arm and beamed. "Let me be the first to congratulate the person responsible for leading the winning team."

"You mean . . . ?" *Please say those magic words*, Lindsey said to herself.

"The board of directors was so impressed with the proceeds from the Elvis show that they've given early approval for the care center!" He grabbed her hand and raised it in victory. "We may be able to break ground even earlier than expected."

Lindsey resisted the urge to give Henry a kiss on his balding head. "But the board hasn't even considered the money from our other planned activities."

"That's what makes this so spectacular! The show

was so wildly successful that we already have enough. The money from the other activities will be the icing on the cake. This is big, Lindsey. Very big!" Henry unloosened his tie and did a little spin. "A move I learned from your Elvis friend."

"Well, you can thank the rest of the committee," Lindsey said. "I was just along for the ride."

"I'm so grateful that I'm giving each committee member a gift certificate for dinner at Lucia's Italian Restaurant. You've all made a remarkable difference and should do some celebrating."

She should have told Henry that her own foolish notions about Jason almost prevented this show from happening. The other committee members came up with the idea. Then Bernie made the first move. Sure, she agreed it was a great idea, but if she hadn't felt pressured, her own pride would have put a kibosh on the whole event. And instead of hearing Henry talk about the success of the venture, she would have been hearing his regrets about the end of the care center.

And she was so tired of regrets.

"Well, that's a wrap for today," Mary said to Lindsey. She snapped off her computer and the screensaver of the town's lighthouse disappeared from view. "Let's clear out so second shift can have all the fun."

Lindsey didn't answer. She clicked the cap on her pen and stared out the window.

"You in there?" asked Mary, jolting her friend back

to Earth. She put away her folders and threw out a crumpled candy wrapper from her desk.

"What? Oh, sorry. I drifted off."

"I noticed. Any place good?"

Lindsey furrowed her brow and put her hand on her hip. "I mean, who is this guy anyway?"

"What guy?"

"Jason. Elvis. Whoever he is. You know who I mean." Her tone was edgy.

"Oh, so that's where you went," Mary said with a slow nod of her head. "Off to dreamland with The King."

Lindsey gestured with upturned hands, sounding more angry than her comment called for. "I mean, he takes care of his brother, takes my grandfather to the dentist, does free shows. Why is he so darn nice? What's up with him?" She tapped her finger on the desk to emphasize her point.

"You're asking me? I don't know. He's just a nice guy." Mary shrugged and held out her arms. "They do exist, you know."

Lindsey sighed, shoulders slumping. "I know he is. I just wish he were a minister or a missionary or a kindergarten teacher. They're good professions for nice guys."

"Well, if his brother had reacted favorably to a man in a white collar, Jason would have probably become a singing priest. That's what nice guys do, nice things."

Lindsey put her hands on her head and moaned. "Ooww, Jason Kincaid is driving me crazy."

"The King has that effect on people," Mary laughed. "You saw what went on at the show."

"What am I going to do?" Lindsey rubbed her eyes.

"Well, it's not like he hasn't given you enough hints about the way he feels. I'm surprised he hasn't given up on you."

Lindsey held her breath. "Given up? You think Jason would give up on me?"

"Why not? Hey, you may be a good catch, but you're not the only fish in Lake Ontario! Women throw themselves at Elvis and wind up in Jason's arms. Not a bad deal."

Lindsey had become so out of touch with everything outside of her career that she'd forgotten how to be part of a relationship, how to be a woman. Sure, she always hoped for that special someone to come around, but she didn't expect him to be dressed in costume! This just wasn't fair!

She plopped down her head on the desk. "I like him, Mary. I really do," she said, her voice muffled on the desk top. "I tried not to, but it happened anyway. Now what?"

"Now you make it work the best way you know how."

Lindsey raised her head and looked at her friend.

"Since you like to keep everything in neat little sensible packages, and you've all but shut the door on the guy, I'd say you have to make the next move. He's obviously too much of a gentleman to get pushy with you."

"You mean, ask *him* on a date?" Lindsey felt her breathing quicken and her throat go dry. "I can't do that!"

Mary looked at her with raised eyebrows. "Well, if you don't, Doctor, what prognosis will you give this relationship?"

Lindsey thought and wrinkled her nose. "Dead on arrival."

Lindsey settled Tom in front of the television for his evening ritual of game show viewing. The kitchen was cleaned up from dinner. She had called her patients and was satisfied they were resting comfortably. She even took the time to sort through the pile of catalogs stashed on the chair. She stood in the living room with her hands on her hips and surveyed the house. There, everything was in order.

Only one more task on her to-do list.

"Grandpa, I'm going to sit on the porch for a while. Such a nice night." She grabbed the phone and headed for the door.

"Ride the wave," said Tom, his eyes glued to the television.

"What?" Lindsey paused.

"Ride the wave, dummy, ride the wave." He pointed to the television, speaking to the game show contestant.

Lindsey looked at the screen and saw Tom's words turn over one letter at a time on *Wheel of Fortune.* She breathed a sigh of relief for the reasonable explanation for his outburst.

He turned to his granddaughter. "You say somethin', honey?"

"Just going outside to . . . ride the wave." She smiled at the prophetic phrase and reminded herself there were really no coincidences in life, only fate taking action.

After her discussion with Mary, she had decided it was indeed time to take the bull by the horns and call Jason. She'd been silly to keep backing away from him. She saw the way he looked at her, the way he focused on no one else in the room but her. She had an inkling, a gut feeling actually, he could be that one special guy she had waited for her whole life. But she'd never be able to verify that if she kept shutting him out. Time to open the door and see who would walk in: Jason or Elvis. Both?

Lindsey sat on the porch under the starlit July sky, complete with a wink from the crescent moon. The delicate breeze was scented by honeysuckles that entwined the fence. The perfect time and place to bare her heart and soul. If she were told to go away, at least she could lean against the porch railing and gaze into the beautiful sky like those actresses in the old movies. Let her heart break for the chance she had wasted as she contemplated her single life.

She took a deep breath and dialed Jason's number. The phone rang three times. No answer. She hung up, hand still on the receiver, and froze. There. That had been easy. She tried, and it didn't work. So now she could move on to other things, other people, or no one at all. Before she had even finished feeling sorry for herself and planning her dismal life as a spinster, the phone rang.

"Hello?"

"Hi, Lindsey. You just tried to call me."

"Oh, Jason. Hi. Yes, I . . . I did." Was he psychic too? A fortune-telling Elvis act. Now that would be unique.

"I saw your number pop up on caller ID. I was on the phone with St. John's. Kevin had a rough day."

"Is he okay?" The doctor was never off duty.

"Yeah, he's sleeping. Sometimes he gets a little out of sorts if he doesn't see Elvis for a couple of days."

Lindsey could relate. "It doesn't take much for people with neurological disorders to get off kilter. Routine is usually very important to people with disabilities."

"The nurse assured me that he's fine now. I was surprised to see your number show up. Need anything? Tom's tooth okay?"

She twisted her curls around her finger and imagined the performance at the dentist's office. "Everything's fine, including Grandpa's teeth. I . . . I just wanted to call and ask . . . ask if you'd like to go to Lucia's Italian Restaurant sometime?" She felt like a silly teenager afraid to approach the cutest boy in the class. Every day she grappled with life and death with an unflappable resolve and an iron temperament. How could she be nervous about asking a guy—one who dressed like Elvis, no less—to go out?

"Sure, I'd love to," Jason said quickly.

"Henry gave everyone on the care center committee

a gift certificate to thank us for arranging your show. Since you're the star, and I really didn't do anything, I felt it only right to share dinner with you." She had to explain, partly to cloak her embarrassment at asking for a date and partly to admit her guilt for hesitating to ask him to perform in the first place.

"Thanks for thinking of me."

If only he knew she couldn't stop thinking of him. She felt warm and anxious, a thin layer of perspiration forming on her upper lip. She had asked him out, and he had readily accepted. The hard part was over, right? "I mean, I could give the certificate to you and Bernie, if you'd prefer." She rubbed her forehead. "I just thought . . ."

Jason laughed loudly. "Now you must be joking. If you weren't part of the dinner plans, what would be the point in going? The chance to spend some time with you is what matters."

She inhaled deeply, composing herself. "You're very sweet, Jason."

"Just say when."

"How about tomorrow night at seven?"

"Can we make it seven-thirty? I have something before that, and I want to give myself enough time."

"Seven-thirty it is."

"As long as you're buying, I'm flying. Pick you up at seven-fifteen." Silence. "Oh, Lindsey, I'm really looking forward to seeing you."

"Me too," she said before they shared final good-byes and hung up.

Lindsey sat in the darkness, the phone still in her hand and a smile on her face. She was going on a real date with Jason. Not a coincidental meeting or an occasion that included his manager and her grandfather. A real evening out between a man and a woman. She'd been on plenty of dates with nice guys, but Jason was different, special. She hadn't felt this excited about an evening out in ages. When she practiced medicine, she often relied as much on her gut instinct as she did on her medical training. And her gut was telling her Jason was someone she needed to have in her life. Now if only her brain would start to agree.

"You still out here?" Tom asked through the screen door. "What's going on?"

"Just riding the wave, Grandpa. Just riding the wave."

Lindsey was in the kitchen at seven-ten drying the last of Tom's dinner dishes when the doorbell rang. She quickly put the towel on the counter and smoothed out the front of her orange blouse so it lay flat over her brown slacks. She straightened the heavy gold necklace around her neck.

"Come in, young fella," she heard Tom say. "Didn't expect to see you tonight. Thought my granddaughter's friend Jason was paying her a visit."

Oh, no. Lindsey's stomach knotted. Please let it be Andrew who rang the doorbell. She took a deep breath and headed into the living room. There, standing in a hot orange bell-bottomed jumpsuit, a close match to her blouse, was Elvis. She was sure Jason was somewhere under that glitter and fluff. Or at least somewhere under the wig. Too bad Lily wasn't in the mood to make a flying leap off the bookshelf onto his head.

"Wow, look at you!" Jason's face lit up as Lindsey walked into the room.

"Hi," she said, trying to hide the disappointment in her voice. The lectures she'd given herself about accepting who people are, not judging a book by its cover, and admiring Jason's gallant reasons for posing as a dead celebrity flew right out of her brain. She and Jason would make quite a splash at the restaurant.

"Are we having a show here?" asked Tom, his eyebrows lowered and mouth puckered as he studied Jason.

"It's just me, Jason, in a costume. Remember we talked about the way I dress up for the shows? When you think you see Elvis, it's really me."

"Well, I'll be," Tom snickered. "Had me fooled, young fella."

Lindsey wondered if she should at least change her blouse so she didn't look like Elvis's sidekick.

"Sorry about the suit." Jason swept his arm down the length of his torso. "I did a show at St. John's for the youth volunteers before I came here. Then I had to spend a little extra time with Kevin to settle him down."

"Is he okay?" asked Lindsey, her throat dry. Why did he always have such a noble reason for his antics? It would be so much easier to dislike the silliness if he were just a goof.

"A couple songs and a little hip movement, and he's happy as can be." Jason's smile captured the relief he felt.

"Glad to hear that," Lindsey said. "Well, we better go." She looked at her watch. They needed to be at the restaurant in fifteen minutes, so they wouldn't have time to run back to his apartment so he could change. No, she wouldn't even suggest it. She kissed her grandfather on the cheek. "Andrew will be over in about a half hour. Don't let the animals out."

"Have a good time, kids," Tom replied. "Bring me home a cannoli."

After the initial flurry Elvis created when they entered the restaurant, Lindsey and Jason were seated at a table by the wall. At least they weren't in the middle of the restaurant. Before dinner was served, a few people came over to ask for Jason's autograph. He obliged with enthusiasm, and Lindsey sat patiently and even forced a smile. As each person left, he apologized for the intrusion.

"You certainly are popular." She was unable to feign excitement in her voice.

"Not me. Elvis. I'm just keeping the fantasy alive." He raised his glass of wine. "To the best and loveliest doctor that Owl Cove has ever had. To *my* doctor."

They clinked glasses, and she felt her cheeks heat up. She looked across the table. Such dark, sparkling eyes. And his smile was so sincere, so warm. Did it really matter that his soft blond hair was covered by that hideous black synthetic matt? Or that he'd traded in his Oxford shirt and khakis for a blinding polyester jumpsuit? She knew the person who masqueraded as Elvis; shouldn't that be enough?

Just when their dinners were served and Lindsey had taken her first bite of lasagna, a middle-aged couple rushed to their table. The woman, her teased black hair reminiscent of a female version of Jason's wig, crouched behind Jason so her head was at his shoulder. The man stood behind Lindsey at the other end of the table and focused his camera.

"Excuse . . . ," Lindsey started to say, turning to the man who was so close she could feel his breath.

"Smile, Rose," the man said to the woman, ignoring Lindsey.

The woman poked Jason's shoulder, almost causing him to choke on the forkful of ravioli he had just put in his mouth. "You smile, too, honey."

"Uh, can we wait until . . . ," Jason began.

The camera flashed in Jason's eyes, causing him to jump, shake the table, and spill his glass of water.

"One more," Rose said, placing her hands on Jason's shoulders and plastering a wide smile on her face as she posed.

Lindsey again turned to the man. "Can you please stop?"

"Would you move a little to the right so your head's not in the way?" he asked Lindsey, his sizeable girth invading her private space.

Lindsey scowled. "Excuse . . ."

"Hurry up," Rose ordered the man through clenched teeth so as not to disrupt her fake smile. "I need an autograph for Aunt Stella too."

Jason held up his hands and stood. "I'm really sorry, folks. I'd be happy to let you take a photo and sign an autograph, but right now I'm eating dinner with my date. Not now."

Rose pursed her lips, and the man lowered his camera with a huff. "Your voice doesn't sound like Elvis when you talk," she said.

"I'm not Elvis, ma'am," Jason said firmly. "And right now, I'm here on a date with this young lady, not doing a performance. So if you're still in the restaurant when we've finished dinner, I'll be happy to let you take a picture. But right now, I have to ask you to stop so my date and I can have dinner—and be alone."

Lindsey sat upright and looked directly at Jason. He smiled, nodding slightly. He'd said date three times. Three times! She really enjoyed the sound of that word. The real intent of the evening was clear to him. And even though she kept telling herself that they were just two friends having dinner, she knew better.

The man and woman slinked away from the table, mumbling to each other.

"I'm really sorry about that." Jason blotted up the water with his napkin.

Lindsey smiled widely. "As I said earlier, you're a popular guy."

"Well, they were a little too pushy. Even The King has a breaking point." He went back to his ravioli.

Lindsey took another bite of lasagna. "That was hard for you to do, wasn't it?"

"What's that?" Jason mechanically reached for his water glass before realizing it was empty.

Lindsey handed him her glass. She'd only taken one sip. And since they were on a date, things like germs didn't count. He nodded thanks and accepted the glass. She felt an odd connection with that water.

"Well, I know how dedicated you are to your fans and to keeping the Elvis aura alive. I can't imagine you turn away too many people."

He shook his head. "I don't. But first things first. And the first thing right now is you. Us." He reached across the table for her hand, resting his fingertips on hers. "Elvis has a lot of fans, but I have only one Lindsey."

She inhaled deeply. She tried to keep her smile to a dull roar, subdue the wide, silly grin that, if allowed to erupt, would tell the world her true feelings. Was she really touching hands with Elvis and feeling a zing inside like she'd never felt before? What was happening here? She and Elvis? No way. She and Jason? Hmm.

"So what was the funniest thing that ever happened to you during a show?" asked Lindsey, needing to make conversation before she went ga-ga right in the middle of the restaurant.

Jason snickered, recalling the incident. "I was doing a show downstate in this outside bandstand. Everything started out just fine. Nice crowd. Nice weather. I was right on cue with the music . . ."

She caught his excitement as he spoke. "Big crowd?"

"I'd guess about five hundred."

"Impressive!"

"No. That made it worse." He raised his hand, his eyes popping widely as he animated his tale.

She furrowed her brow waiting for the story to continue.

"Out of nowhere, and I mean nowhere, this tornado-like wind started, knocking branches off the trees, blowing over lawn chairs. It was like *The Wizard of Oz*!"

"No flying monkeys, I hope!"

Jason pointed at Lindsey. "I knew you were a closet comedian. I would have hoped for a flying monkey! This huge gust blew right onto the stage and sent me on my backside, taking my wig with it. Kind of like when your cat rearranged my hair."

Lindsey grimaced. "Sorry about that again. Then what happened?"

"Well, my pride was more wounded than my behind, so I got right back up and looked out into the audience. Instead of scattering from the storm like I thought they would, most of them just stood there, mouths gaping, looking at me. By this time, the worst of the storm had blown through and I was ready to keep going with the show, wig or not. Then out of the corner of my eye, I saw some little old guy, like your grandfather, totter onto the stage, wearing my wig."

"No way!"

Jason nodded rapidly. "The crowd was howling! I started the music, and this guy stood there, singing and swaying like it was nobody's business. The little bugger completely stole my show."

Lindsey smiled at the glow on his face as he recounted the incident. "You weren't upset that your show was ruined?"

"It wasn't ruined, just altered. The audience had a good time, and that's my measure of a successful show."

Another valiant reply. "Ever think of performing as just yourself instead of Elvis?"

Jason shook his head. "Naah. In time, I'll have to return to my career as an accountant and put the performing behind me. I've always known that. But right now, Elvis has a magic Jason could never have."

Lindsey grasped his hand. "I think you're wrong about that."

Chapter Thirteen

"Where is everyone today, Mare?" Lindsey approached the nurses' station and set some charts to be filed on the desk. "Not that I'm complaining, but all we've had is the sequoia-sized woman with the bloody nose and the cute boy with appendicitis." Lindsey took out a small notebook from her pocket and scribbled on it. "Reminder to check on him when he's out of surgery. He's in good hands with Enrique."

"Hope Enrique doesn't play guitar for the poor kid!"

"Might work better than anesthesia!"

"So are you going to keep me in suspense about dinner last night?" Mary sat back in her chair and cradled a steaming mug of coffee.

Lindsey walked behind the desk and poured herself a cup from the hissing pot on the table. She leaned on the end of the table and faced Mary. "It was great." The corners of her mouth turned upward.

"Details, details," Mary demanded, motioning with her hand.

Lindsey felt a little shiver at the memory of her date with Jason. "Well," she started, unable to contain her smile. "Dinner was very good."

"I don't want to hear about the food. What about you and The King?"

Lindsey sighed. "Well, when he showed up at the house dressed like Elvis, you could have knocked me over with a feather. Not good. I just resigned myself to go to dinner and get the whole thing over with."

"Don't tell me he wore his costume!" Mary's shoulders slumped. "Oh, no."

"My reaction exactly. He was running late from a show at St. John's. I'm cursing the guy in my head, and then he tells me he was performing for some group of volunteers at the nursing home and spending time with his brother. So you can imagine what kind of a heel I felt like." Lindsey shook her head.

"So was it weird? Having dinner with Elvis? In public?" Mary's eyes were wide with anticipation. "I mean, he's adorable, but . . ."

"Sitting across the table from Elvis was weird, but the real Jason shone through. That was the wonderful part. He actually told some autograph hounds to back off because he was on a date." She couldn't suppress the smile that popped on her face. "Not just a casual dinner. A date!" she repeated, the excitement raising her voice an octave.

"He's got it bad," Mary replied. "To think he was so excited to see you he didn't even run home and change. He'd rather risk being seen in his costume than miss one minute with you. How romantic." She placed her hand on her chest, raised her eyes upward, and sighed. "That type of guy doesn't come around every day, you know."

Lindsey flicked away Mary's comments with her hand, but she savored her words like piece of rich, dark chocolate. "He was just being nice."

"And you have it bad too."

Lindsey pursed her lips and shook her head. She wasn't ready to admit everything, not even to her best friend.

Mary raised an eyebrow. "Just tell me one thing. By the time dinner was over, were you still bummed out by the Elvis factor?"

Lindsey thought for a moment. "Guess I'd stopped noticing."

Mary stood and met Lindsey eye to eye. "I rest my case."

Suddenly, they both jerked their heads toward the ER entrance when the commotion of incoming people blotted out the silence. "Peace and quiet is over," Mary said, grabbing a clipboard of blank forms and hurrying with Lindsey to the door. "It's show time."

Lindsey skidded to a stop at the doorway. Holding

his own arm and being led by a teenage boy and a middle-aged woman was Jason. The woman watched him intently, her face filled with worry, touching him gingerly like he was a carton of eggs.

"What happened?" Lindsey hurried to Jason, placing a hand on his shoulder.

He smiled when he saw her. "Really, nothing. I'm fine. Hi, Mary."

Mary cocked her head at the sound of his voice. "Jason?"

He nodded.

"I never saw you without your costume." She looked at Lindsey, raised her eyebrow, and nodded in approval.

"I was teaching my son to drive," the woman said, motioning to the boy. "This nice young man was standing on the corner, waiting to cross, and Craig took the corner too close. I hope he's all right," the woman added, her voice shaking with distress. "Oh, my."

"Were you hit by the car?" asked Lindsey, unleashing a panic in her voice that she never let her patients see.

"No, no, no. I was startled by the car and jumped backward, right into the streetlight. Hit my elbow. The zing from my funny bone had me hopping on one foot for a few seconds." Jason rubbed his elbow and winced.

"I'm really sorry, mister," the boy said, looking at the floor.

Jason smiled at him through his pain. "You didn't do anything wrong, pal. Nothing that a little driver's ed class can't fix."

The woman wrung her hands and her face twisted. "He seems fine now, but I was so worried that he'd go home at night and end up with some blood clot, hemorrhage, or organ rupture. How could I ever forgive myself if that happened?" she said to Lindsey. "I just read on a Web site about a woman in China. Everyone thought she had a cold, but it turned out to be some form of a plague. A whole village had to be quarantined. You just never know what could happen!"

"Don't believe most of what you read," said Mary.

"Really, ma'am. I just bumped my elbow. I'm fine," Jason emphasized.

"I insisted he let us drive him here to be checked out," the woman continued, still addressing Lindsey. She took a deep breath and then asked in a quivering voice, "Do you think he'll make it?"

Lindsey looked at Jason and grinned. He rolled his eyes and shrugged. "He'll be just fine. Appears to be just a little bump, but I'll check him out."

"I hope you're right," the woman whined. "Really, Craig meant no harm. I'm just a terrible driving teacher. I hope I don't have to do time for this."

"These things happen," Lindsey replied. "Try not to exaggerate things. All's well that ends well."

Mary handed Lindsey the form with notes she'd been taking. "How about if I get you a cup of tea so you can relax a little," Mary said, taking the woman's arm and leading her toward the waiting room, the boy following behind. "We'll leave the doctor to take care of our patient." Behind the woman's back she raised her finger to her head and made a circular motion while mouthing the word *cuckoo.*

"I've never seen anyone quite so high strung," Jason said when the woman was out of earshot. "I told her I was okay, but she was on the verge of a breakdown. I had no choice but to get in her car. People were starting to gather on the corner!"

Lindsey led him into an exam room. "You're a brave guy to get in the car with her!" she said as she settled him onto the chair. "Let's have a look at that elbow."

Jason's short sleeve gave a clear view of the bruise that had already formed. Lindsey poked and prodded, asking him to move his arm in several directions. Other than a little cringe when she pressed directly on the red spot, she didn't see any problems.

"I don't need another x-ray, do I?" he asked.

"No, you're good." Lindsey uncapped a jar of ointment and rubbed some on his elbow. "This should help case any muscle tension in the area."

"Feels great," Jason said, closing his eyes while a little smile flashed on his face. "I was going to stop by to thank you for dinner, but I had hoped to do it in a little more, uh, dignified manner." He opened his eyes wide.

"Well, you have become one of our regular customers," Lindsey joked. "Too bad we don't have a frequent flyer program. I'd much prefer to see you in a restaurant than in one of these exam rooms." By the time the words were out of her mouth, she was already wishing she could stuff them back in. She was finding it harder and harder to mask her feelings for this man. "Thanks for your company last night. I had a really nice time."

"Sorry about the costume and the annoying fans." He leaned closer to Lindsey. She continued to rub the mint-scented ointment onto his elbow, circling the bruised area with gentle strokes.

"Well, I have to admit that as much as I don't want to see you show up here as a patient, I was glad to see the real Jason walk through the door this time. How's that?" She flexed his arm to test the muscle tenderness.

"Much better. You have an extraordinary touch. It was worth taking a hit on the arm to get a little extra attention from my favorite doctor. We've progressed from holding hands to holding arms!"

Lindsey wondered if her cheeks were red to match the heat rising from under her collar. "Now, let's not mix business with pleasure," she said with an exaggerated wink.

"Say, how about if I make up for last night and take you and Tom to Rudy's for a fish fry tonight? That's one of my favorite spots, right on the lakeshore. We can sit at a picnic table, throw rocks in the water, and dodge the seagulls. I'll see if Bernie wants to join us. You heard that woman. What if I break out into some terrible rash or my head falls off? I'd sure feel better knowing my doctor is with me." He grabbed Lindsey's ointment-covered hand. Standing, he took her other hand.

She restrained herself from saying yes to his invitation right away. "No costume?"

"No costume and no fans," Jason said with a quick dip of his head.

"I'm a fan."

"I'd like to think you were more than that," he responded.

"Perhaps that could be arranged," Lindsey said, realizing that her doctoring had just segued into flirting.

Lindsey lit the citronella candle on the porch although there were no insects. A candle always enhanced the ambience, even one meant to repel the bugs. She turned to see the flame flickering in Jason's eyes, picking up the golden hue of his hair. She positioned herself on the swing next to him, hiking up her legs and hugging her knees.

"I sure didn't need ice cream after that huge fish sandwich," Jason said, patting his stomach. "As my doctor, don't be shy about warning me about the dangers of cholesterol."

She laughed. "I'm the one who should feel guilty. After eating all that dinner, I ate a hot fudge sundae! You only had a cone."

"As if you have to worry!" Jason smiled. "What do you weigh? Maybe a hundred pounds?" He poked her side with a playful finger.

"In my dreams!" Lindsey wasn't used to receiving compliments on anything other than her medical skills.

So he had been paying attention to her figure. Suddenly, she was grateful her work kept her running at warp speed most of the time to offset the occasional sundae she indulged in. "Listen to those two in there," she said, changing the subject and pointing toward the screen door. "You'd think Grandpa and Bernie were actually playing for the prizes on those game shows, the way they're yelling out answers."

"Keeps the brain sharp. Better that than those celebrity gossip shows."

Lindsey raised her eyes. "Speaking of celebrity gossip, don't you think you've stirred up enough around here?" she teased. "Owl Cove never had so much excitement until Elvis came to town."

"I'll let you be the judge of that," he retorted with a twinkle in his eyes. "Unfortunately, in my line of work, gossip and publicity go hand in hand. Hope it doesn't bother you when people talk about Elvis dating the doctor."

Lindsey perked up. She and Jason may have had a date, a couple outings together, but she didn't think they were dating. Dating meant that they saw each other exclusively. She hadn't agreed to that. Not that she wouldn't. Dating meant her family and friends would see them as an item, always ask one about the other. She'd done her best to not publicize her interactions with Jason. Mary was the only one who knew, and Grandpa still couldn't fully decipher if Jason and Elvis were one or two people. She and Jason hadn't even shared a good-night kiss, not for lack of trying. Despite it all, he seemed to think they were . . . dating.

But if they were actually dating, which Lindsey didn't think they were, would that be so bad? Yes, she thought it odd for her—or anyone for that matter—to date an Elvis impersonator. Dating Jason would certainly be an attractive prospect, but the jury was still out on dating Elvis.

Her throat felt tight, and her mouth was dry. She reached for the ice water on the table. "Are we, you know, dating?"

He squeezed her hand and delivered a question-infused smile. "Would you be open to that?"

She turned away from his penetrating gaze and hesitated. This was her defining moment. If Jason and his Elvis act were more than she bargained for, she could tell him right now. Put an end to the speculation and indecision. Then he and Bernie would leave and not return, unless Jason had another accident and ended up back in the ER. Or she could . . .

Lindsey entwined his fingers in his and raised her eyes. "Yes, I'd be open to that," she replied, her voice quiet.

As Jason moved closer, his lips approaching hers, Bernie appeared at the screen door, waving his cell phone. He cleared this throat, causing Jason to jerk back his head.

"Sorry for the interruption, kids, but I got big news," Bernie said, walking onto the porch, the door flapping behind him.

"News?" asked Jason.

Lindsey inhaled deeply and told herself the news had better be good to make up for the kiss Bernie interrupted. She was beginning to doubt they'd ever share a smooch.

"Just got a call from Bally's in Las Vegas." He hesitated, and a huge smile covered his face.

Jason's eyes grew wide and his mouth opened.

"You're in the Elvis contest! You made it, son!"

Jason released his grip on Lindsey's hands and jumped to his feet. "Are you kidding me? I made the contest?"

"Heard it with my own ears," Bernie said. "Here we go. One step closer to the big leagues."

"I can't believe it!" Jason took Lindsey's hands, hiked her to her feet, and hugged her quickly. "And to think you're here to share the excitement with me."

"W-what excitement w-would that be?" she asked, wrinkling her nose as she perused the mile-wide smiles on the men's faces.

Bernie pumped his fist. "A few months ago, we heard about this big contest that Bally's does in Vegas every year for Elvis impersonators," he explained. "To enter, you have to send a film of yourself performing. From all the entrants, they pick the top ten. Those ten finalists and their managers are invited to go to Vegas, all expenses paid, to perform before a live audience who votes on the winner."

"They get thousands of entries," Jason added through his smile. "And to think that I'm one of the ten." He and Bernie shared a high-five.

"Wow!" said Lindsey, failing to catch the genuine thrill that Jason and Bernie shared. There had to be something she was missing. "That's awesome."

"The winner gets a hundred thousand dollars and a one-year contract to perform in a lounge at Bally's," Bernie continued. "We're one step closer to saying hello Vegas, good-bye Owl Cove."

Lindsey caught her breath and stood straight. She snapped her head to Jason and locked her eyes on him. The air suddenly became very still, deflated. Good-bye Owl Cove?

Bernie cleared his throat. "I'll be going back inside," he said softly.

For what seemed like an eternity, neither said a word. The darkness grew denser and the distant chirps of crickets appeared to be much louder than they actually were. Surrounding them was the hum of cars passing in the distance, voices from passersby, and the rumble of a jet in the sky. But their world was silent.

"This is a wonderful opportunity," Lindsey finally said. "I'm very happy for you." She forced a smile.

Jason leaned closer to her. "I'm sure it will end up to be just a nice little vacation in Vegas. The other nine competitors will have this sewn up. Jason Kincaid from Owl Cove is pretty small potatoes."

Lindsey's heart broke as she watched the hope and excitement drain from his eyes. "Not in my book."

Lindsey walked out of the exam room, reading a chart as she hurried. She looked up just in time to avoid colliding with Bernie. "Now what happened to him?" she asked, reaching for his arm.

"Mornin', Doc," Bernie drawled, holding his rain-soaked cap. "Nothin' wrong with Jason."

She placed her hand on her chest and exhaled loudly. "Thank goodness. I mean, it's been almost a week since he's been in here for some calamity." She put on her glasses and looked at Bernie. "You feeling okay?"

"Despite the shower that turned this lovely summer day into a monsoon, I'm just fine. Do appreciate you askin'." Bernie scuffled his foot. "Wonder if I might have a word with you?"

Lindsey furrowed her brow and removed her glasses. "Sure. Come in here." She led him into an empty exam room and closed the door, her nerves on end. "What's wrong?"

Bernie scratched his head and pursed his lips. "Jason would have my hide if he knew I was here."

So something was wrong with Jason! Lindsey felt the panic rise from her toes to her throat. "What?" she asked quickly.

"Well, you know he won that contest to perform in Vegas."

"Yes, yes."

"You saw with your own eyes how excited he was to hear the news." Bernie nodded slowly and smiled slightly.

"I'll say. Like a kid at Christmas. So what's the problem?" She leaned on the bed.

"He said he doesn't want to go now." Bernie looked her in the eye and shrugged. "Got me concerned."

Lindsey raked her fingers through her hair. "Why the change of heart?"

"Well, Doc," his voice slowed and quieted. "He's afraid he'll win."

Lindsey let out a little laugh that Bernie didn't share. "Well, that's why people enter a contest, with the hopes of winning. Why doesn't he want to win?"

"There's more to it," Bernie continued. "If he wins, he'll need to move to Vegas for a year. And then, who knows, maybe longer." He raised an eyebrow and rotated his hat by the brim.

She took a deep breath. A year away from Jason. Really, the start of forever. Their relationship could end even before it had a chance to start. She'd been so foolish to let these last few weeks go by as she wrestled with herself. Of course Jason was the man for her. She'd been so blinded by his costume, wig, and peculiar profession that she'd failed to see what really mattered: a man whose love for his brother had led to a touch of good fortune, much less than he deserved, but still enough to make him truly happy. In the middle of it all, she failed to see—really see—the man she loved.

Lindsey fingered the sheet on the bed. "That shouldn't

stop him. He needs to follow his heart, follow his dream."

"'Fraid that's what he's doin'," Bernie replied.

"I don't understand."

A grin crept onto Bernie's face. "Jason found his dream right in his own backyard. He found you."

Lindsey swallowed hard. What could she possibly say to that? She didn't want Jason to go. She wanted him to remain in Owl Cove with her, build a relationship with her, find happiness with her. But she would never ask him to forsake something he'd worked years to achieve. He had to pursue his big break—even if she wasn't part of it.

"I'll talk to him," she said quietly, closing her eyes.

"Thank you. I'm sure you'll say the words he needs to hear."

When her shift ended, Lindsey called Andrew and asked him to fix dinner for her grandfather and sit with him until she came home. She reminded him to keep Tom inside so he didn't get a chill from the rain. Then she drove to Jason's apartment, her fingers crossed that she'd find him home.

As she walked up the stairs to his apartment, her legs felt weak. She helped patients and their families make decisions every day, decisions that could change the course of their lives forever. So why couldn't she convince herself that the right choice, the only choice, for Jason was to go to Vegas? He'd knock the socks off everyone who saw him. And he would stay there for a year. And then forever. If he left, she'd never see him again. But if he stayed, he'd sell his heart to a doctor who, until now, couldn't even pull herself together enough to realize how much she cared about him.

She knocked quietly on the door, holding her breath until he answered. "Definitely a surprise!" Jason said, placing a hand on her arm and guiding her inside. "So you're my rainbow on this rainy day."

"Hi," Lindsey said, not sure how to even begin the conversation. "Miss Downing's flowers will really be sprouting after all this . . . ," she started, her words coming to an abrupt halt when she noticed his costumes laid on the cushions and back of the couch, a large suitcase open on the floor. She sighed. So he'd already decided to go. She really didn't need to be here after all.

"So what brings you out on such a wet evening?" he asked.

"I came to . . . to wish you good luck on your trip to Las Vegas." She glanced again at the costumes. Three wigs sat on forms on the coffee table. If she hadn't stopped over, would he have left without saying goodbye?

"Thanks, but I'm not going."

"But you're packing." She motioned to the costumes with a sweep of her hand.

"Yeah, I'm packing all right. Putting these things in storage." His face darkened, and he lowered his eyes.

"Storage?"

"Yeah, I've given up the act. Elvis has left the building, for good."

Lindsey gasped at his words. "But what about Vegas, the contest, your career? What about Kevin? What happened to all of that?"

Jason placed his hands on her shoulders, squaring her to him. "You."

Lindsey didn't reply. Couldn't. She felt no joy at all in knowing he was ready to give up everything that had defined him for his whole life for a woman who'd been too foolish to accept him for who he was. Even if that woman was her. She shook her head slowly, fighting tears.

"If I win, I'll be away from you for a very long time. And if I stay here and keep doing these bit acts, I'll turn you into the doctor whose boyfriend is Elvis. Neither is good for you, Lindsey."

A tear rolled from her eye, and Jason caught it with the tip of his thumb. "But they're good for you. And Kevin. You can't give up your dream. Or your brother's dream."

"I can put on a wig and sing to Kevin at any time, and he'll be happy. Why, I can even take him on a trip to Vegas sometime, sing to him there. But you, Lindsey, there's no way I can be Elvis and be yours. We both know that."

"But you and Elvis are responsible for the care center, for making so many people smile. Everyone in Owl Cove would love to see you make it in the big time, become famous for their sakes. There are so many people who love you."

"But there's only one person whose love I want." He slid his hands down her arms and reached for her hands, holding them tightly.

"I won't let you sacrifice for me," she said through her tears. "I just won't."

"Sacrifice? If you'd agree to be with me, it would be a blessing, not a sacrifice." He looked at her, his eyes deep and probing. "Will you?"

Lindsey's eyes darted to the bookcase. She saw the childhood photos of Jason and Kevin, the smiling boys in the truck, coaxing her, forcing her to come to terms. She glanced at the costumes. It was all here, just waiting for her to decide. This little apartment, just a stopover for better things, seemed way too small to hold a man bursting with so much promise, so much desire.

"No," she said, her voice barely an audible squeak.

Jason tilted his head, his face twisting with question and confusion.

"No. I won't be your . . . your girlfriend, part of your life. Even if you stay here. Go to Vegas because we won't be together, here or any place. Just go."

With all the strength she could muster, Lindsey released Jason's hands and headed for the door, not turning to look at him and the life she'd just discarded.

Chapter Fourteen

"Come on, Lind," Mary coaxed, laying a gentle hand on her friend's arm. "Henry put out all kinds of goodies in the cafeteria to celebrate the official announcement of the care center. You know he especially wants the committee to be there."

Lindsey spun around in the chair behind the nurses' station. "I just don't feel like celebrating. Bring me back a cookie."

"Maybe a little mixing will do you good." Mary sat in the chair next to her. "It's been a week."

Lindsey grabbed the sides of the chair and tensed her body, tilting back her head as if to contort herself into someone else. "A week that's seemed like a year. I can't believe how much I miss him, even his crazy wig. What

I wouldn't give to see him walk through that door right now with another one of his bruises."

"Didn't think it would hurt this much, did you?"

Lindsey's eyes filled with tears. "When I told Jason I didn't want to have a relationship with him, he wasn't the only one I was lying to."

"If you could, would you take back your words?" Mary pulled up the Internet on her computer and typed while Lindsey stared at the ceiling.

"No," Lindsey replied. "As much as I want to be with him, he had to go to Vegas. I couldn't live with myself if I stomped on his dream. Not just his dream, but his brother's too. He's worked a lifetime for this chance. He needs a better reason than me to give it up." She sniffled and a tear ran down her cheek.

"Well, maybe he had to go, but that doesn't mean you have to stay."

Lindsey turned to her friend whose chubby cheeks had dimpled with a mischievous smile. "What?"

"Look," she said, pointing to the computer screen. "Here's Bally's Web site. The contest is in two days. If you leave tomorrow, you'll get there in time to see it."

"I can't go to Las Vegas," Lindsey whined. "I mean, come on. Vegas?"

"Why not?"

"I just can't go there. J-just . . . go. Can I? Vegas?"

"Well, you haven't taken a vacation in three years, so you certainly have the time."

"What about Grandpa and the animals?" Lindsey's mind was rumbling with excuses, something to shed some common sense on this situation.

"Andrew can take the day shift, and I'll take over throughout the night." Mary smirked. "Told you I owed you one from when you nursed me through that flu last year."

Lindsey's eyes darted as her thoughts ran wild. "But it's so expen—"

"It's summer, not as many tourists, better deals. Play the slots a little and the casinos will even comp your lunch." Mary looked at her deliberately, ready to field the next excuse.

Lindsey shook her head. "No, I couldn't." She shook her head again. "No." She sat still for a few seconds, and her mouth turned up at the corners. "Well, maybe . . . maybe I could."

The women stood, joined hands, and jumped like schoolgirls. "Book my trip," Lindsey said. "I'm going to Las Vegas!"

By the time the taxi dropped Lindsey off at Bally's, the hundred-degree heat, even at ten in the evening, and the ocean of people had her swooning. She was fanning herself with a coupon booklet that a man on the street gave her as she waited to register at the hotel.

"Just one?" the clerk asked, stretching his eyes into inquisitive slits, as he verified her reservation.

"Yes."

"This can be a lonely town for a single woman."

"I'm meeting a friend. Elvis, actually." She gave a sharp nod of her head, realizing how right those words sounded.

The clerk smiled politely. He'd no doubt heard that before.

Lindsey went to her room, turned the air-conditioning to HIGH, and unpacked. She contemplated calling Jason's room, but she had no idea if he even wanted to see her. That was a possibility she'd been trying to prepare herself for. If she showed up at his room, he may tell her to take the next plane back to Owl Cove. Then he would be in a terrible frame of mind for his contest, and she would be responsible for ruining his chances. He didn't deserve a double whammy. She'd already done enough damage. No, she'd just show up at the contest and enjoy him from afar instead of getting in his face.

That would put fate in the driver's seat because she had no idea where she was going.

At noon, Lindsey made her way past clanging slot machines, people cheering at the roulette wheel, and more blackjack tables than she'd ever imagined existed to get to Bally's convention center for the competition. As she expected, people were already arriving for the one o'clock show, and she wanted to get a good seat. She'd seen enough of Jason in pain and in good spirits to know what emotion to look for on his face.

She landed an aisle seat in the third row and congratulated herself on this small victory.

The audience was filled with men, women, and children who wore Elvis T-shirts, glasses, fake sideburns, and full-blown costumes. One remarkably heavy man wearing a red, white, and blue cape held a sign that said "Elvis for President." Some local and national news stations were in attendance to capture the whole bizarre event for the rest of the country. Apparently, the grave was no match for Elvis's popularity.

Elvis songs were piped into the convention center, pumping up the audience for the upcoming extravaganza. Lindsey saw from her program that Jason was to be seventh to perform. *Lucky seven*, she thought. How appropriate for Vegas. Her excitement took on an edge of anxiety when the house lights dimmed and the announcer asked everyone to silence their cell phones in preparation for the show. "Come on, Jason," she whispered. "Show your stuff."

Following a blast of introductory music from the band that stirred the already hyper crowd into a frenzy, the first entertainer, a man from Wichita, took the stage. He swayed and dipped to "Hound Dog," and Lindsey had to admit he was very good indeed. She would have bet money that his hair was his own, not a wig, which made her think he fell into the questionable segment that considered themselves to be Elvis in body as well as mind. The crowd went wild when he ended his number by turning his back to the audience and sweeping his caped arm into a wide arc before flicking his hand at the exact final beat of the song.

The next five performers were all just as impressive but each unique in his own way. Different songs, different moves, same results: a fun show eerily reminiscent of the real man.

As number six ended his song and said, "Thank you. Thank you very much," the cadence of Lindsey's heart took on a life of its own. Jason was next. Her nerves swelled. She placed her hands into a prayerful steeple over her lips, waiting, waiting to see the man who had stolen her heart perform like the celebrity she'd come to know—and love. She wanted more than anything for Jason to get on that stage and blow away the competition. She knew he could do it. She just knew it. She'd seen him perform, and he could hold his own against any of the performers she'd seen so far. They were all formidable entertainers, but only one was *her* Elvis.

The curtain lifted, and the introductory measures of "Blue Suede Shoes" resounded over the hushed audience. Under blue lights, Jason faced the audience and plunged into his act, the lights transforming to a colorless brilliance. The crowd clapped and stood, and he reacted to their energy. He didn't miss a beat. Every note was crystal clear, every move expertly executed. To anyone who didn't know Jason, hadn't seen him perform, he was a dead ringer for The King himself.

Only someone who knew his heart could see something was wrong.

Lindsey studied him. That look she'd seen at his other shows was missing. That deep, personal serenity—singing first for himself and then for his audience—wasn't there. He smiled and charmed to perfection, but that subtle spark she'd seen embrace the crowd in his other shows was missing.

Jason wasn't happy on that stage.

Lindsey saw Bernie standing by the side of the stage. He rubbed his chin and watched Jason perform. He lowered his head, shaking it slowly from side to side, his lips pursed.

When Jason stepped down the middle of the stage into the audience, the crowd clapped and whistled. His flawless singing continued while he placed scarves from his neck on some women who screamed, cried, and crumbled at their brush with the legend. They buried their faces in the strips of fabric, breathing deeply, as if those dime store scarves were the keys to their existence. Perhaps they were.

Lindsey's heart beat rapidly and longingly as Jason approached her row. Singing, facing the opposite end of the auditorium, he mechanically removed a white scarf from his neck, then turned to her. When he saw her, the notes of the song kept coming and his smile widened so that she wondered how he could sing through that grin. He kissed the scarf and gently placed it around her neck, brushing her cheek with a gentle sweep of his hand. She ushered the scarf to her lips and also kissed it. Jason stood before her, lingering longer than he had in front of the other women, reaching to touch her arm as he sang.

His eyes flickered under the theater lights, and when he turned to continue his number, his hand slowly released from her, as if he struggled to let go. With his eyes still on Lindsey, Jason hopped back onto the stage.

He finished his number with a gusto and verve that the first half lacked. His face was serene and satisfied, and the audience absorbed him. The spirit Lindsey had come to cherish had returned. For those few moments, he was Elvis. And she knew then that he would forever be her Jason.

Bernie looked over and winked at Lindsey. Tears rolled from her eyes as she watched Jason finish his act with the enthusiasm and passion that he cultivated within himself. The crowd shared the love he emanated.

He owned the stage—and her heart.

Chapter Fifteen

Lindsey fingered the scarf from the concert as she waited for Jason in the hotel lobby. With her head still reeling from the show, she was almost oblivious to the bustling surroundings. Not until a rude bellhop wheeling an overstuffed luggage cart said, "Get out of the way, lady," did she pay attention to the zoo-like atmosphere she was smack in the middle of.

This was the perfect climax for the blur that the last few weeks had been. As she reflected on that whirlwind, she could come to grips with meeting an Elvis impersonator and falling for him in a way she never thought possible. But the last thing she ever expected to do, for Jason or any man, was travel across the country and surprise him. That was way out of her comfort zone—or at least the comfort zone the old Lindsey had.

She looked up to see Jason emerge from the elevator. He wore khaki slacks and a button-down Oxford shirt with the sleeves rolled up to his elbows. Cool, pulled together, and simple. Classic Jason. As soon as he saw her, an enormous smile popped on his face and he waved. Her heart skipped a beat. She and Jason were two explorers who'd uncovered their buried treasures in each other.

He greeted her with a warm hug and a quick kiss on the lips. "This feels better," he said, tugging at his shirt collar. "You can get pretty warm in those costumes." He took her hand and they walked out onto the busy strip, walking slowly in the hot evening.

"Good thing you changed," Lindsey said, flashing him a sideways glance. "You've already caused quite enough of a stir. Can you imagine what would happen if you wore your costume on the street?"

"Probably nothing! Elvis sightings here are just as common as the sun." He laughed.

She cleared her throat. "Disappointed?" She felt nervous to broach the subject.

He shrugged and tilted his head from side to side. "Yes and no. I came here with the hopes of winning, especially when I didn't think my future would be in Owl Cove, but something changed that."

"What?" asked Lindsey.

He put his arm around her. "As soon as I saw you in the audience, I knew I'd already won my prize." He gave her a little squeeze. "I still can't believe you're here! What made you come?"

"I had to." Lindsey lowered her eyes. "I . . . I couldn't stand myself, leaving us like I did. You needed to be here, and with me in the picture . . . it wasn't going to happen."

"So that brilliant breakup performance was just a ploy to get me to go to Vegas?"

Lindsey flashed him an apologetic smile. "Pretty slick, huh? Would you have gone otherwise?"

He shook his head. "I would have given up the contest if it meant I could be with you." He leaned close and whispered. "I never imagined I could have both."

They walked along in silence for a few minutes, letting themselves get carried away by the lights, sights, and sounds. They ignored the people who urged them into their shows and restaurants. The creative street beggars dressed like priests and holding signs saying they'll work for food didn't even register. There was only each other.

"I know I'm biased, but you were the best one." Lindsey wanted to be sure Jason wasn't depressed that he'd lost the contest. "You really were. I mean, the guy from Wichita who won was good, but he didn't hold a candle to you."

"You're just saying that because you're relieved I didn't fall off the stage or trip over the microphone cord." Jason put back his head and laughed heartily.

Lindsey joined his laughter. "Well, I'm certainly glad you refrained from any accidents. Good thing your doctor was in the house." She stopped and looked him in the eyes. "You really are a remarkable talent, and I'm sorry I didn't always act supportive of your career choice. I'm sorry I couldn't see past the costumes and the wig especially!"

"You cure; I perform. Everyone is called for a different purpose. People's choices aren't meant to be understood by others, just themselves." They continued walking.

"You should have seen Bernie's face as you ended your number," Lindsey said. "He was just beaming. I could hear him yelling and whistling. That sight alone was worth the trip."

"He's a great manager and a friend. I hope we can stay in touch when I quit."

Lindsey halted and grabbed his arm. She furrowed her brow. "Quit?"

"It's time," he said with a deep sigh. "I did what I needed to do. I promised Kevin I'd perform in Vegas for him, and I did. I have a DVD of the show to play for him whenever he needs to see it. I fulfilled his dream, and one of mine."

"There are lots of opportunities for Elvis impersonators here," Lindsey said. "Seems like a clone of Elvis is on every street corner. You didn't have to win the contest to be successful."

Jason shook his head. "I'm a CPA. Guess it's time to get a *real* job."

"What does that mean?" She inhaled deeply, not sure where the conversation was leading. Knowing exactly where she wanted it to go . . .

They stopped and ordered two lemonades in plastic glasses shaped like lemons. Lindsey sipped through the long straw, her eyes on Jason.

"I'm sure there are a lot of CPAs in Vegas too," Lindsey added, puckering her lips from the tart drink. She wasn't trying to convince him to stay; but if he chose to go home, it had to be all his idea. Of that she was sure.

"One of the nice things about accounting is that it can be done anyplace. Vegas, New York, even Owl Cove."

Lindsey felt a chill despite the blazing temperature.

"What do you think of Vegas?" asked Jason.

She looked around. "A little overwhelming, actually. Excess at its finest. I can't believe how many people gamble!"

Jason smiled. "There's really a lot more to Vegas than the casinos."

"Like what?"

"Food and shows, to name a few things."

"True," she commented. "Sure are enough restaurants here."

"Shopping," added Jason.

"More stores than anyone could ever need."

"And there are . . ." He pointed to a small white building decorated with oversized, illuminated flowers around the door. A neon flashing sign said WEDDING CHAPEL.

Lindsey's eyes darted from the chapel to Jason and back to the chapel.

"Until I met you, Lindsey, I wasn't sure where life would lead me. I never knew how much was actually missing from my life until I found the thing that was absent. You."

She took a deep breath, but her lungs seemed small and the air seemed thinner than she remembered it being just a minute ago.

He turned to her, took her hands in his and raised them to his lips, gently kissing her fingertips. "Lindsey, I love you."

Her eyes filled with tears. "I love you, too, Jason."

He raised his hand to her cheeks and cupped her face gently, his touch oddly cool and comforting on her burning face. "Do you really? Despite all the shenanigans with the Elvis thing? Do you really love me?"

Tears formed in her eyes. "I . . . I came here to find you. To find myself. To be with you. Since I met you, my life has never been zanier, more complicated, and . . . and more wonderful. Yes, I love you."

He placed his hands on her shoulders and pulled her closer. "People in love should be together—don't you agree?"

She nodded, unable to speak.

"I mean, together officially, in a place they can call home. In a place where their families reside. A place like Owl Cove," Jason continued.

Lindsey smiled. "That's where we should be. Yes, home, together."

An impish grin crept on his face and his voice raised with excitement. "Then let's do it. Let's be together. Officially, I mean."

Her eyes widened, and she waited for him to continue, shed some light on this obtuse conversation.

"Let's get married."

"Married?" She placed her hand over her mouth, covering a little gasp. "Married?"

Jason nodded, his eyes bright with anticipation. "Lindsey, will you marry me? We can go in there right now and make it official." He pointed to the wedding chapel.

She glanced at the flashing light that beat in sync with the tug-of-war her heart and brain were playing. Married! Being impulsive wasn't her style. Dr. Lindsey Bartlett didn't do things like date Elvis impersonators, travel to Vegas on a whim, and—most of all—get married on the spur of the moment. Well, she'd already done two out of three. And she was in Las Vegas, after all. If she'd been a gambling woman, she'd bet this was a good place to make it a full house. She thought for a few moments. "Yes and no."

Jason tilted his head.

"Yes, I will marry you. But not there," she said, gesturing to the chapel with a flick of her head.

"Then where?" asked Jason.

Lindsey pointed to another chapel across the street.

An oversized sign in front said THE KING WEDDING CHAPEL. GET MARRIED BY ELVIS. "There," she said with a smile, entwining Jason's hands tightly in hers and leaning so close she could feel the beat of his heart. "It just wouldn't be a wedding without Elvis."